FIREBIRD

FIREBIRD

K A WILLIAMS

For Leslie

K A Williams

ISBN: 987-0-692-13346-0 (Hardcover)

Any references to historical events, real people, or real places are used fictitiously. Names, characters, and places are products of the author's imagination.

Front cover images by Kristen Williams.

Book design by Kristen Williams.

Printed by IngramSpark™

kawilliams.sales@gmail.com

For my sister. You deserve so much more.

1

CAGED

———

"Raise hell," they told us.

I suppose you could say that's what we did. There was fire, and the devil kicked up a fuss. I remember quite a lot of religion. I remember people screaming while it burned. I remember diversity with the feather-bright thoughts of a child, where the world's catastrophes were bookmarks for my own life.

But mostly, I remember people louder than myself. I sat with my friends, my neighbors. I listened to my mother, furious with the religious leaders. I remember my brother. He screamed at the television, his face purple, his eyes scared. And afterwards, we'd continue existing, surfaces within a bubble of quiet. The rest of the world burned, and we were in a position to watch it happen.

I went to college in the Fall of 2990. It was the year they patented BioMage. And it was the year of Unity.

I hope that you never know an era like mine. I hope that you never know that life just keeps going on, even though the bodies are piling up. I hope that you never know the numbness humanity contains, the complete disregard for life, the ease with which you can stop thinking of a person as a person.

I did my undergrad studies at a local college, in a small town in northern of-then America. You've probably never heard of it. America, that is. Because, like I said, the year I went to college was the year of Unity. And after Unity, there were no countries.

There was just, you know, the one.

We thought that it was mankind's greatest leap forward. We had, at long last, Earthly peace. All cultures were boiled down, the nuts and bolts of society becoming cogs in a great machine of mankind.

Here's the problem with a revolution. What do you do with the people who disagree?

Unity's solution was simple. It was the same conclusion our species has come to since the time of the hunter-gatherers. It's just that instead of spears, Unity had science.

Unity had BioMage.

We did not kill the opposition. Not all of them, at any rate. BioMages have trouble with some people, some part of their DNA that reacts differently. Those people, we were told, had to die. For the greater good, of course. They were going to be rewarded, of course. Of course, we could do nothing to help them.

Unity was not a war; it was an idea. BioMages were not soldiers; they were a religion. They converted a world.

It's just that instead of having a god behind them, they had science. And here's the thing with science: you don't need faith, not when you can rewrite a person's brain.

"*Yar* Lurkshire?" he said.

I gave a start, flicking my tablet off. There was a moment, my fingers laying numb on the smooth, black screen, when my spittle turned to acid. I was contained. I swallowed my panic. I closed my tablet. I looked up at the officer and I smiled.

"Yes?" I asked, focusing on his eyes—a soft kind of green—instead of the metal badges on his grey uniform.

"We're ready for you, now."

He had a good kind of voice. The soft kind, the kind that pops up in childhood, a favorite friend's father. Warm and distant, far enough above you that you don't have to worry about competing.

I drew a slow breath, gathering my things, tucking them into the olive-colored satchel at my hip. I was old school, like that. I was one of the few people who still bothered with books, still wanted to feel the dry pages, smell the ink, the memories of sunlight and grass.

Unity did not mind personality. They preferred it, in fact. Every soul is unique, every life a spark in Unity's boundless universe. We were encouraged to be ourselves.

So long as our 'selves' remained within the parameters of what Unity considered a person.

"What's she like?" I asked, waiting as the little machine beside the door scanned his eyes.

The Guard headquarters in Capitol Delta was as hulking and grey as its name would lead you to believe. We were on the nineteenth floor. I'd been waiting for three hours now in a little room with a wall of windows on the north side. There was a reception desk. Literally, a square built in the center of the room, surrounded by uncomfortable chairs, that spoke for itself with a surprisingly lifelike voice. If they knew anything in 3010, it was how to build a gracious robot.

"Pardon?" the Officer asked, opening the door and ushering me through.

"The Firebird," I said, excitement frothing in my chest. "Have you met her?"

"No, *Yar*," he used the title like a reflex, quickening his pace to walk at my side. "My clearance is Level 4."

"Oh?" I feigned surprise. "What Level is Firebird?"

"10, *Yar*," he grinned, and I could see a boy within the uniform.

"Isn't that the highest level?"

"Yes," his grin widened.

"It must have been something, seeing her brought in."

He puffed himself up. I smiled.

"Sure was," he said. "I remember when she made her first raid. I was sixteen. Took down some Unity helicopter, rode it right down and then blew up a hospital or something."

January, 2992, Sector 19, Sector X Hospital, multiple casualties. Suspect: Unknown. Connected to later incidents. Deemed the "Firebird" by local newspaper.

I nodded.

"I remember. I was in college."

"Must have been studying to be a writer," he grinned at me, pleased with his deductive reasoning.

"Then it was just generals," I replied. "I graduated from a little community college, before going on to of-then Oxford."

"That's Sector 97, isn't it?"

"It is," I smiled.

"Did it change much? After, I mean?"

I shrugged, something heavy tugging at my chest as we walked down the white corridor. There were windows on the right, flanked by heavy doors. Everything was a shade of grey: ceiling, walls, doors, floors and uniforms. Some of the rooms we passed had tenants, prisoners with vacant stares sitting on whitish cots. Some had Guards, writing on near-black tablets. Some of the Guards wore the protective visors, the kind patented shortly after BioMage, the kind that covered every part of the eyes, a bit of the brow, and the temples.

"Like everywhere else, I suppose," I didn't touch my forehead, between my eyebrows, though an eye-shaped piece of my skull ached with a dull throb. "Some parts."

The world had been bleached. Nothing was the same, and yet everything was. It was like a dirty kitchen, suddenly scrubbed to sparkling purity. There was no flour on the counters. There never would be again. Unity had the too-clean feel of a building ready to be sold, a home become a house.

"I grew up in Cleveland," he said, stopping at the end of the corridor, letting a second scanner have at his eye with a red beam. "Don't miss it one bit."

He laughed as the door buzzed open. I smiled. I couldn't drum up a convincing laugh, not with my guts twining into fever-tight knots. We continued. He talked. I pretended to listen.

Levels 1 through 3 were quiet, save the soft *clap-tap-clap* of our shoes on the polished floor and the *Yin*'s endless voice. I stopped looking in the cells. They made me feel lonely, a little emptier inside. When my escort delivered me to the Level 4 Guard, he shook my hand. Wished me luck. My fingers were numb.

Levels 4 through 9 had a tighter feel. My new Guard was a blond woman with a tight bun and a tighter mouth. I was grateful for the quiet. I organized my thoughts, focused on the floor, let the monotonous data run seamlessly through my mind. I tried to slow my heart, but it was intent on setting a hard pace. The place between my brows continued to ache.

Level 9 ended differently. We were at the very center of the building. There were no cells on Level 9, only thick, seamless white walls. The door was heavier. There was no scanner. There was no window. I could hear my heart in my ears, feel it in every extremity. I swallowed, tucked a hand against the reassuring thickness of my satchel's strap, and looked at the escort.

"Did you meet her?" I asked as we waited.

The Guard looked at me with cool eyes. Her bone structure was from of-then Norway, her clear eyes skeptical and sharp. She nodded. Just once. Her mouth was a line as thin as the seam of the security door we waited in front of.

"What's she like?" I asked, pulling my tablet from my satchel, smiling. "I'd really like to have a few different viewpoints for my article."

The Guard hesitated at that. It's funny, the effect a record has on people. They didn't need to know that I'd never forget a detail, with or without my tablet. And even for the ones who did know, there was something different about having your words put into print.

It put her back up.

"She's a prisoner," she stated, as textured and colorful as the lifeless walls.

I nodded, jotting it down with my stylus. She frowned at me. I looked at the bars over her heart, making sure she noticed my glance, before smiling at her and snapping the tablet closed.

"That's an excellent attitude," I said, slipping the tablet back into my satchel.

She glowered at me. I've never met someone who could scowl for ten minutes straight, but there's a first time for everything. When the security door finally buzzed, it was not to admit me. Instead, a small shelf rotated out of it. Laying on the cold, grey panel, there was a visor.

"You will wear it at all times," the Guard said, taking the visor from the tray and holding it out to me. "If at any point you remove it, you will be forcedly removed and blacklisted."

I nodded, turning the grey metal in my hands. No matter how many times I held one, I was always surprised. First, by the heaviness. The main component of BioMage Bands was lead, of course. Second, the visors were cold—but in a strange, lingering way, less like they were kept in a freezer and more like they *were* the freezer, chilling from the inside out, *emanating* cold.

I fitted the visor over my eyes, pressing the center firmly against the place between my brows. The back of the visor was gel-like, and it fitted itself to the unique contours of each face. The ache dulled. I secured it over my temples. The world around me quieted.

I hated it. I could *taste* the metal, feel its aching chill pulsing against my skull. I was as uncomfortable as it was possible for me to be.

They were not shaded. They were solid, and yet I saw as clearly as I had without the visor. The technology was exceptional. BioMage Bands converted what I would be seeing and projected it directly into my eyes. If powered down, I would be looking into the black nothingness of a lead-lined strip of metal.

The Guard inspected my handiwork, ensuring the visor was fixed properly. When she was appeased, she stepped back, offering me a severe nod.

"When I am gone, the door will let you in. After your interview, you need only stand before the door and it will allow you exit. You will at no point touch the prisoner. Any contact will terminate your visit and you will be blacklisted. You will be closely observed and recorded. Before exiting the building, you will be informed on what information may be publicized. Any information leaked will be promptly destroyed and you will be blacklisted, pending prosecution as a Level 10 security threat. Should your questions vary from the pre-approved list, you will be blacklisted and placed in custody, pending a Level 10 security hearing. Do you understand the aforementioned limitations?"

"I do," I answered, my grip twisting on the satchel's strap.

The Guard nodded, snapped off a perfect salute, turned on a heel, and marched back down the length of the seamless corridor. By the time she exited, back to the safety of Level 8, I was sweating in earnest.

I turned to the door. My heart hurt, it beat so slowly, so firmly. I swallowed, feeling numb within the limitations of my visor. Everything looked the same as before, just as clear, just as real. But *something* within the visor was always lacking. Life was too sterile. I swallowed.

Quiet filled the hall. Like lead. *Quiet fills the hall like lead.*

The door buzzed, and I flinched. There was no handle. It simply swung open, seamless and perfect, and a wash of cool air spilled around me. And suddenly, I was not alone. And nothing was sterile. And the world clipped into perfect stillness as I stepped into Level 10, numb with the security of a woman who knows she's about to die.

2

BIOMAGE

"Oh, fuck me," I breathed.

The room was white, of course. The ceiling was round, a perfect dome ending in the perfect circle of the floor. Unity liked circles. Every skyscraper built after 2990 was round.

The Firebird sat in the center of the room.

The chair was grey, with manacles built into the frame. They clasped her wrists and ankles, biceps and shins, thighs and waist. She could turn her head, but her neck was cuffed to the back of the chair. Her fingers could move, but each one had a white clip around the end, little green dots over each nail. She was in a skin-tight, white leotard. It was nearly transparent. Apparently, her rights to privacy had been revoked along with those to movement.

Her eyes were nearly black, and they fixed to me like a reptile's.

There was one other chair in the room, and I was strangely relieved to see that it was devoid of restraints. My hands were shaking. I kept one on the top of my satchel as I sat across from her. My spit had decided to turn to ash, and so for a solid minute, I simply stared at the Firebird.

She had short, black hair. It was messy. Her nose was hawkish, her skin the color of burnt sugar, and her face was marred by countless pockmarks. She did not scowl at me. She regarded me with those nearly black eyes, shaded under thick brows.

I could see coils of muscle move beneath the leotard, tensing and relaxing. Tensing and relaxing. Like the gills of a fish out of water.

She would have been described as Native American, once. Before Unity. Before the world's borders were erased and all nations and nationalities became *of-then*.

I offered the Firebird a smile, but it felt fake and flimsy and it wilted on my lips like a flower dropped into acid. Her stare was crushing me. No, not her stare. She could have been blindfolded and I still would have felt the invisible *hand* upon my soul. I resisted the urge to touch the visor, to ensure that it was still in place and therefore my secrets secure.

I cleared my throat.

"My name is Jezi Lurkshire," I began, still gripping my satchel's strap. "I work for the Sector X *Truth*."

The Firebird did not offer her name. Not that I expected her to. She was a wraith, after all. I felt myself sweating, felt the cool dampness in my pits, and made a mental note not to raise my arms. I spent a moment wishing that I would have worn black, not red. Then, giving my head a brisk shake, I opened my satchel and began to pull out my tablet.

"You will not need that," the Firebird said.

I gave a start, dropping the tablet. It missed my satchel and hit the floor with a dull *thump*, the little black screen bared as its cover flopped open. I stared at the

Firebird. She hadn't shouted, but her words struck a cord within me, like a parent's command.

"I'm," I cleared my throat again, still reaching into the empty air, as though to catch the fallen tablet, "sorry?"

The Firebird stared at me for a moment longer, and I could feel a bead of sweat crawl from my hairline.

"Are you?" she asked, quirking a thick brow.

She had a strong voice, deep and rich. She spoke clearly, enunciating each syllable with weighty certainty. She did not stare at my visor, where my eyes would have been. Instead, she watched my mouth.

"With your permission," I began again, stooping and picking up the tablet, "I would like to conduct an interview for our newsletter. Should you comply, I would like to record our conversation," I tipped the tablet toward her, as though proving its innocence.

She was quiet for a moment, muscles flexing.

"You do not need the tablet," she said again. "I know you, Jezi Lurk."

I stared at her, felt my heart stumble.

"You do?"

The Firebird dipped her head, eyes remaining on my mouth.

"Who are you named after?" she asked me.

It was my turn to pause. I glanced up, at the round, black camera at the center of the domed ceiling. These were certainly not on my list of preapproved questions. But, I wasn't the one asking them, was I? I shifted on my chair.

"My mother," I shrugged, trying another smile.

"And who was she named by?"

I shrugged.

"Her mother, I suppose. Honestly, I don't know."

"My point being," and the Firebird tapped all ten fingers in rapid succession, "we never choose our names. They are given to us. And we build ourselves around them."

"I suppose that's true."

"I know who gave me my name, Jezi."

My hands froze. The ash in my mouth turned to acid once again, and I didn't even attempt to swallow the panic. My heart took flight. My face felt numb.

"You do?" I whispered.

The Firebird eased back, looking more comfortable than any woman chained to a chair had a right to be. The heavy silence pressed into the room again. I shook my head, crushing my tablet against my thighs.

"Is that how you would like to be referred to, then?" I eventually asked. "As Firebird?"

"That is who I am," she answered.

"So, you read my work?" I felt the strangest flutter, something deep in my chest.

"Devoutly," flexing, relaxing, flexing, relaxing.

"Well that's," *careful, Lurk.* "That's fascinating. Really. So, would you be willing to allow me to interview you?"

"Very."

"Oh," my hands trembled, just a bit, as I turned my tablet on. "Oh, that's wonderful. *Yo* Firebird—"

"Just Firebird," she corrected. "And you will not need that."

Again, she looked at the tablet.

"But, Firebird," I frowned at her, "you said that you're willing to allow me to conduct the interview?"

"I am."

The lights in the little room flickered. Just for an instant, just for the space of my heartbeat, like a hummingbird's blink. She had a wide, thick mouth, like two fingers. One side of it twitched. She cocked her head.

"Your eidetic memory will suffice for the duration of our interaction. And you may remove the visor. We both know that you do not need it."

Oh God, I felt my eyes widen uselessly behind the visor. *Oh God, oh God, oh God*. The blood rushed from my face, leaving me pale and sweaty. I'm pretty sure that my heart just stopped. I looked again at the camera in the ceiling and felt like weeping. Every part of my body, every nerve and every cell, tensed, waiting for the metal door to buzz open and banded Guards to come pouring in.

"No need to panic, Jezi," Firebird said. "They cannot intrude."

"How," my voice was a lifeless rasp, and I swallowed. "How do you know?"

The Firebird sighed, and it was as heavy as the silence.

"I am a devout reader. I have noticed you, through your writing, through your observations. Particularly through the rare television interview you have shared, Jezi, I have noticed you. I have, shall we say, a keen eye for Mutes."

"Oh, fuck," I breathed, the tablet dropping from my lap and smacking the floor, like a dead thing.

I wanted to cry, then. I wanted to curl up in a tight little ball, right there on my tablet, and *scream*. So many years, so many lies, so many lives all unraveled in so *little* time. I should not have come. I had known that from the very beginning, hadn't I? Even before I had named the Firebird, I had known that I should keep silent. I should have watched the world burn.

"As I said, they cannot intrude," Firebird rolled a wrist.

Suddenly, the manacles around her wrists, ankles, thighs, shins, biceps, and neck sprang open. I flinched at the sound. And then I gaped. I looked again at the camera, at the little red light blinking away. I looked at Firebird. She sighed, heavier this time.

"I detest not seeing a person's eyes," she said. "Remove the visor."

"They said I would be blacklisted."

"They *cannot* intrude. And even if they could, the things that they do to Mutes is infinitely worse than being blacklisted as a writer. Remove the visor."

It no longer was a request. Even through the lead on my forehead, I could feel her presence, could feel the weight against my third eye. I wanted to weep for the pressure of it.

I reached up, pushed in the little buttons behind my ears, and the visor released me with a gentle pulse of air. As I peeled it away from my face, I squinted. The white lights around the base of the room were brighter without it, the visor having filtered down their severity.

"That's the problem with blinders," Firebird said as I blinked. "They choose what you see."

And I met her gaze. Something slammed against my skull, a presence like I had never known before, and I gasped, covering my third eye reflexively with my hand. It felt like she was splitting my forehead with an axe.

Of course, what else was I to expect, meeting the unfiltered gaze of the most powerful BioMage in the world?

3

FIRE

"You are strong," Firebird said, still sitting as though the shackles hadn't been opened.

"Jesus Christ," I said, falling forward, my knees cracking against the cold floor, clutching my head.

"My apologies."

The pressure shifted, fading to the subtle, prickling awareness that I was not alone. I looked up, trembling. Firebird stared back, quiet and curious.

She was not as I had seen her. Her nose was swollen, blood dried under one nostril. She had a black eye, her lower lip was split, and the bruise shading her right jaw was all shades of blue and yellow. She did not wear a leotard. She wore nothing at all. There was dried blood on her knees, her knuckles, her chin. She looked like she had been dragged from the mangled remains of a car wreck. The clamps on the ends of her fingers had blood actively running from them.

"My God," I breathed, blinking at her, so stark and feral in the artificial, blinding light of the horrible room. "What have they done to you?"

"Much less than they would do to you, as a Mute," she said, cocking the bushy brow again. "Particularly one as powerful as yourself."

I got to my feet. The room made me dizzy. Or maybe that was the BioMage. Or the sense of impending doom.

"How do you know that they can't see us?" I asked, looking reflexively at the camera.

"I am a BioMage," she said, as though explaining why animals needed air.

"But that doesn't mean you can control a fucking camera. Biological creatures, only. And these walls are too thick, even for you. Besides, who knows where the security team even is?"

"I assure you, they are inconvenienced to an extreme," she looked down at her hands, at her bleeding fingers within the clamps.

"What do you mean?"

"They are locked in their room," she snorted through her hawkish nose, and blood misted down her front. "Jezi, I must ask something of you."

I swallowed, still trembling a bit, and looked at the security door. It was as quiet and closed as ever. I looked back to her.

"What?"

"I need you to remove these," she raised her hands slightly, the clamps still showing little green lights. "And once you do, several things will happen in rapid succession. I am not quite myself," she gestured to her bruised and bloodied body, "and I may need your assistance."

"Assistance with what?" I asked, approaching her warily, the hair rising on the back of my neck.

"Escaping."

I paused at that, though it wasn't really a surprise. After all, the Firebird had never been successfully held by

Unity. Oh, they'd come close. I remembered every near-disaster. I remember clutching my hands together, panic flooding my mind.

The lights in the room flickered again, and I saw the muscles under Firebird's tanned skin tense.

"If you would," she raised a hand, the cords attached to each finger tightening, pulling her back down to the chair. "We're on a tight budget."

"I can't help you," I said, something inside of me cowering. "I don't know what makes you think that I can."

"Jezi," and she gave me a stern, knowing look. "I know everything about you. You are the reason I'm here."

"I'm the—"

"But I'd sooner kill you myself than allow you to endanger my team. As it is, once the security team escapes, you will be destroyed."

I scowled at Firebird.

"Why do you want me? If you're just going to fucking kill me," I said. "What's the difference?"

"Between being killed and being destroyed?" there it was again, that almost-smirk.

That was when the alarms began to go off. The light in the room flashed to red, and the screaming sirens down the hall made my heart stumble awake. The floor itself vibrated with them. I slapped my hands over my ears, eyes watering. Firebird continued to regard me.

"What'll it be, Jezi?"

With a helpless scream, I threw myself forward, taking one of her hands and narrowing my eyes at the clamps.

"This is un-fucking-believable," I whispered, tugging experimentally at one of the things.

Firebird flinched.

"Pry the ends open. There is a needle within. You do not have the strength to pull them off."

I gripped the open ends of the jaws and found that they opened rather easily, though requiring two hands. My stomach did an uncomfortable, loopy kind of thing when I saw the long, bloody needle remove itself from her fingernail.

"Jezi, you should move a little more quickly," Firebird said, looking as disinterested as a fish.

"Fuck me," I breathed again.

It did not take long for me to remove the clamps, though the phrase *vomit later, vomit later, vomit later* was unhelpfully running through my brain. When she was free, Firebird took a deep breath.

"Help me to my feet, if you would?" she asked.

I was still swearing when I pulled her arm around my shoulders. She was heavier than she looked and smelled strongly of blood and sweat, but as she put her weight against me, we moved with surprising speed. No sooner had I slowed for the door, question poised on my tongue, than it sprang open with a welcome rush of fresh air.

I didn't bother asking how she managed that, nor why the next nine doors were open. The hallways were empty, and several of the cells that I passed had Guards within them, their shrieks of outrage soundless in the thickly padded hallway.

We exited the first Level and I was once again in the empty waiting room. Red lights glowed and the sirens wailed, but the elevator's lights were out and the screen that should have displayed the buttons for it was black. I looked at Firebird.

"Now what?" I asked.

She was leaning heavily against me, and her dark eyes fluttered half closed. She gripped my shoulder with a sweaty palm and nodded to the wall of windows.

"I would prefer that we get behind this desk," she said, sinking to her knees and dragging me along with her, putting the reception desk in between ourselves and the window.

"*Welcome to Floor 19*," the helpful little receptionist robot chimed, "*authorities have been notified of your presence, please have a seat.*"

"Why are we—" I started.

There was a sudden, muted, insistent humming. I frowned, leaning around the edge of the desk. My jaw dropped.

There was a goddamned spaceship outside. Not a hovercraft, not an airplane. It filled the windows, and as my eyes focused, I realized I was staring down two guns the size of small shuttles. Emblazoned across its nose, written in crimson, big-ass calligraphy, was the word *Redwing*. Firebird grabbed my arm and jerked me back behind the desk a moment before the world *exploded*.

4

FLIGHT

"JESUS!" I screamed, my hands flying over my ears, my body squeezing into the smallest possible ball.

Glass shattered, bullets ripped through the top of the desk, *dissolved* the waiting room's chairs, thudded into the thick wall across from me. The sirens wailed endlessly on. Debris turned to shrapnel, and I saw rather than felt several pieces slice the meat of my bicep. I rotated, pressed to my side in the fetal position.

Quick as that, the gunfire ceased. Truly, it couldn't have lasted longer than a few seconds. But to me, a lifetime had been spent.

"Rise," Firebird said, pushing herself to her feet.

I wasn't trembling—I was vibrating. I couldn't hear. Not really, not through the ringing and the buzzing and the cotton-stuffed brain my skull now contained. I wobbled upright, tripped on something, and hit the ground, something sharp in my satchel stabbing my abdomen.

By the time I'd managed to get to my knees, we were no longer alone.

Two women sprang from the ship, jumping through the ruins of the window wall. Glass shattered under their heavy boots. They each carried a gun approximately the size of my thigh, and they scanned the room with the efficient motions of soldiers. When their guns paused on me, my hands shot reflexively over my head.

The first was tall and heavily built, her armor a complicated mix of Unity and Martian technologies. Her helmet's visor was open and cool eyes regarded me. When she saw Firebird, still standing behind the ruins of the desk, her pale mouth thinned.

The second was tall, thin, and lightly armored. Within the delicate-looking helmet, her face was as black as Phobos, the whites of her eyes like the peak of Olympus Mons. She grinned.

"That mod!" the thin woman exclaimed, kicking a bit of destroyed robot-desk and slinging her rifle—*Level X Automatic, acid-based*—across her back. "Brute has outdone herself."

"Oh my God," I managed. The thickly built woman turned to me and I felt myself shrink under her stare. I shook my head, "You're them."

"Who the fuck else would we be?" the thin woman grinned at me.

"Ori," Firebird said, hands held in front of her chest, fingers lax and bleeding.

"Right," the thin woman—Ori—said.

She stepped to Firebird's side, reaching for her arm. Before she got there, the second woman made a dismissive gesture at her—a motion that slapped the visor down on Ori's helmet—and strode to Firebird. Easy as I would flick a stray crumb from my blouse, she plucked Firebird from the ground, cradling her like she would an infant.

"Always one for the social graces, that Regina," Ori said, voice mechanical within the helmet. "And you can put that on the record."

"Brute?" Firebird asked as Regina carried her toward the ruins of the window wall.

"Still in the core," Ori said, offering me a hand.

I accepted it. The synthetic plating was cold and rough against my skin. She gave my back a heavy pat.

"This the one?"

I swallowed, looking at Firebird. Regina turned slightly, so that her commander's reptilian eyes could regard me. Her thick mouth twisted.

"Take her."

Simple as that, Regina jumped from the window. The toes of her boots must have been magnetic, because when she touched the edge of the spaceship's doorway, she fastened there with a too-heavy *bang*. The doorway, strangely black, swallowed Regina and Firebird.

"Right then," Ori pushed me toward the windows.

I didn't intend to recoil. Really, I didn't. I'm not afraid of heights. But when I looked down those nineteen floors to the white sidewalk below, when I felt the ripping wind from the spacecraft plow into me, when I felt my body give a shuddering urge to just *fall*, I windmilled my arms and clung to the nearest thing.

"Easy," Ori said, grinning a strangely white smile within the dark helmet, patting my arms—which were now securely fastened around her torso. "Just hang on."

"No no no no no no!" I shrieked as the woman squatted, preparing to spring.

She laughed. And she ignored me. I barely had time to wrap my legs around her before Ori leapt out the window.

I lost all sensation in my ass. It's a weird thing to say, and I don't imagine most humans are prone to it, but there it is. When I looked down those nineteen stories, with nothing but Ori's cold armor to comfort me, terror ripped up my legs and fastened to my ass.

Despite being a slender woman, Ori's boots collided with the spaceship with the same unearthly ring that Regina's had. I lurched forward, my grip breaking, and when I fell into the ship, it was like passing through an airy membrane. I gasped as I went, and there was no air.

A sucking sensation, like my skin was in a vacuum. And then, I hit a hard floor. The lighting was warm, the air was a little too hot, and I struggled for a moment with my lungs—which seemed to have forgotten how to operate.

Ori slid through the membrane. She rapped the side of her helmet with a long finger. The visor rushed back and she dropped to a knee, hoisting me up by the shoulder with one hand and slapping my back several times with the other.

"Sorry," she said as my spasming lungs jerked in a rush of air. "It can catch you off guard, if you're not expecting it."

"Trying to kill this one, too?" A woman ran up the hallway toward me, short and thin with a stork-like neck.

"Hush now!" Ori shouted in return, grinning. "She's made of sterner stuff, I'm sure."

The armored woman hauled me to my feet.

"Aren't you?" she asked, cocking a skeptical brow.

The ship shifted, distant engines humming, and I put one hand against the warm wall. My guts were too light, my lungs burning for no good reason, and my insides felt like I had just chugged three cups of coffee in under a minute.

"I'm not sure what's wrong," I gaped at her, tried to take a step, and found my foot was about ten pounds too light. I stumbled into the thin woman and she swore, dropping a white bag marked with the red cross.

Ori laughed, wrapping an arm around my waist.

"You'll get used to it. And we'll get you adapted before long."

"Adapted?" I flinched when the woman's armored fingers dug into my ribs.

"We prefer the Martian atmo to Earth's," Ori explained, hoisting me closer as she walked. "But, of course I do—being Martian. The rest of these babies are just adapting. Too many hours off planet, I suppose."

"Off planet? Martian atmo? As in, Mars? But Firebird is Earth-based."

Ori snorted.

"Sure, she is," she rolled her eyes.

"Stop!" the stork-necked woman snapped, scooping up her bag and grabbing Ori's shoulder.

"Later, Ravin," she said, easily shaking her off. "We've got to get her to the cockpit."

"*Doctor* Ravin," she snapped. "And there's no reason for you to not let me prep her," the doctor scrambled after us.

"Firebird is reason enough," Ori shot her a look.

She scowled, but couldn't argue with that. The spaceship swept past me in a blur, all heat and red-tinged walls. Faces peeked at me from within work stations. I didn't get a good look at them. The floor tilted again, and Doctor Ravin swore.

We reached a room of glass. Or something like glass. The floor was strangely sticky, and Ori's combat boots made squelching sounds as she escorted me to the forefront of the cockpit. Firebird stood near the center, leaning heavily on Regina.

"When did you lose contact with her?" Firebird asked.

A woman of medium build with dark blonde hair sat in the pilot's chair, hands on an old-fashioned airplane's yoke. She wore a tan shirt with the sleeves ripped off, the tattoo of a phoenix flexing on the thick muscles of her bicep. Her eyes were narrowed, mouth thin, and when she spoke, she did not turn.

"Seven minutes ago," the pilot said, her accent something from of-then Australia. "I'm pulling in."

Something dissolved within me as I watched the nose of the spaceship turn, the vessel easing earthward, Unity's building rising before us like a bleached behemoth. The ship angled and I snatched at Ori's arm to keep from falling, my feet stuck to the floor. Firebird's jaw tightened.

"She's never late," Ori said, fear tickling the back of her words.

"Time?" Firebird growled.

"Three minutes," the pilot whispered.

A pause.

"Take us in," Firebird said.

"Fuck no," Regina snarled, reaching for the back of the pilot's chair, as though to rip her from the seat.

"We're not abandoning her," Ori's voice rang too high in the narrow room, the whites of her eyes visible in a halo around her irises.

"We are if it means us getting blown to hell!" Regina turned on Ori, raising a sausage-like finger at her.

"You'll be getting there one way or the other," Ori said, flashing her white teeth.

"Quiet," Firebird snapped.

And the room fell to deathly silence.

Sweat beaded along the pilot's hairline. She circled the ship around the tower, keeping its nose pointed at the sparkling windows, edging lower. We were so close to the building, I could see the white, startled faces of Guards and civilians looking out at us. There was a little girl, in her button-down, grey gown, and she waved before a Guard snatched her wrist.

The screens on either side of the yoke suddenly came alive with red lights. There were no sirens, no audible warnings of any kind, but suddenly, the pilot twisted the yoke and the ship turned on its side, sweeping violently around the building. A second later, seven Unity helicopters unleashed a volley of fiery bullets at the empty air where we had been a second before. Several *popped* against the glass of the tower, sticking there like flies in a spider's web.

"Two minutes," Regina growled, bracing herself against the back of the pilot's chair with one hand and securing Firebird with the other.

"Hands off," the pilot said, voice soft and calm.

Regina released the chair.

There was another burst of speed and the *Redwing* shot sideways, avoiding another volley, and then—with a sickening lurch—the ship darted forward. I think I screamed. I know that when I fell, my knees became strangely adhered to the floor. The world's muted colors whirled beyond the windows. Ori crouched beside me, a manic grin stretched across her dark face, and when the ship came to a shuddering halt, I felt bile rise in my gut.

A burst of static came from Regina's shoulder, followed by a savage cry. I could see only the side of the pilot's face, but when she grinned, it was fierce.

"Must have been jamming the com," Ori said.

By the time I managed to struggle to my feet, the pilot was swinging the tail of *Redwing* to the side, slowly rotating the world and edging under what looked like a flat, black shelf. I blinked.

"Are we *inside* the building?" I asked, jaw hanging.

The shattered remains of a window wall dangled as evidence around us. Little desks and tablets popped and ignited as *Redwing* shifted, wings destroying the government building as surely as a toddler could destroy a doll's house.

"Brute!" Regina shouted into the com on her shoulder. "Move your ass!"

Another burst of static. Then:

"YAAAAAAAAHOOOOOOOOOOOOOO!"

Streaking down from an air vent in the ceiling of the building, there came a thing that most resembled—to my mind—an oversized, pink volleyball. A hurricane of scrap metal and smoke followed after it, like a robot's belch. Ori barked a laugh.

Somewhere deep in the ship, there was a thrumming *pang*.

"Got her," the pilot said, pulling the yoke and nosing the ship toward the hole she'd made in the building's side.

"Punch it," Firebird said, eyes narrowed at the radars beside the yoke.

They were nothing but red dots, swarming like an irritated bee hive, and as my eyes moved to the windshield, I saw them. The better part of a regiment hovered just outside the building.

"Punching it," the pilot said.

There were two levers on either side of her chair, each with triggers and a red button near the top. Between her legs, there was an old-style joystick. The pilot gripped each lever, flipped a plastic cover from the red buttons with twin flexes of her thumbs, and with a deep breath, she shoved both levers forward, thumbs coming down on the buttons in unison.

I'd expected a burst of speed. Instead, *Redwing* shivered. The world outside the windows rippled. And, suddenly, we were not in the building. We were not, in fact, anywhere at all. There was blackness: inky, warm, and vast.

"What," I tried to say, but there were no words. There was no voice. I had no mouth.

A second passed in limbo.

And then, the world flashed back, the com exploded with another war cry, and *Redwing* shot forward. Instead of firing on us, Unity's ships were darting to the side, as though looking for something. The side windows of the cockpits were screens, a high-tech sort of rear-view mirror, and I saw the government building shrinking behind us.

"Three," someone on the com said, "two...BOOM!"

Small as it was in the glass, when the 19th floor of the building exploded, it bathed the rest of the Sector's city in a flash of *white*. They hadn't blown up the tower. They'd incinerated it. Fire curled out of the floor, rippling toward the sky.

"My God," I breathed.

"Not on Unity's Earth, there isn't," Ori said.

"We've got Dragons," the pilot said.

Two black dots marred her radar screens, even as the red faded. Regina swore. Ori's grin soured. And I shivered, staring in the rear-view windows. I could see nothing but a shrinking world behind us. The ship shivered again.

"Preparing for jump," the pilot released the red buttons, plastic protectors clicking back down.

Instead of blackness, white light exploded around my eyes. I couldn't breathe. It was like I'd been immersed in an ice bath. It winked away as quickly as the black, but it left me simultaneously sweating and shivering.

"Clearing atmo in five," the pilot murmured, pulling several latches down from the ceiling, eyes flicking to the rear windows.

I saw something, then. Like the air behind us was caught, moving an image in speed with *Redwing.* Then, they rippled. Twin black ships appeared, the cannons on either side of their cockpits burning orange.

"Harry," Regina hissed, teeth gritted, eyes flashing from the pilot to the rear windows.

"Three," Harry said, the ship vibrating, her arms tensing, hands on the levers and joystick clenched between her knees.

"We don't have—" Ori started.

The black ships released twin, orange beams.

Redwing screamed. The ship quivered, smoke rolling out behind us, and Harry the pilot bared her teeth and snarled. The black ships twisted, side by side, and began turning the beams in a scissor-like motion, clearly meaning to cut us in half.

"BURN ME!" the pilot shouted.

And she punched the levers forward.

5

CAPTURED

When Mars was terraformed in 2190, several things happened in quick succession. First, the Russian areologist who discovered Martian technology disappeared, and an organization called Unity sprang up in his place. Martian tech was hoarded. It had changed a world, after all, and technology became worth more than lives.

World War IV was quick to follow. It was known as the War for Mars, but in truth, it was the battle for Earth. Because when it ended, when Unity nuked the major cities of the world, Earth was what had lost.

A few hundred years of anarchy followed. Unity, broken under the yoke of their own power, was unable to control the factions. Countries still existed, life continued, but it took centuries for the governments to reform. By the year 2800, the factions had transformed into nations, once again dividing the world.

The first Martian settlers were Russians. They landed on one of Mars' two moons—Phobos—in 2880. And in 2881, the first man breathed unfiltered, Martian air.

He died, of course.

It took another ten years before settlers could try again. The scientist Aika Ito realized that it wasn't Mars that needed to evolve, but rather humanity. She had such confidence in her own technique that she was the first one to undergo the procedure. She adapted herself, accelerating her own evolution.

She was the second Earthling to breathe unfiltered Martian air.

And she was the first BioMage.

After that, Mars could be settled. And, not unlike the gold rush in the old American West, Earthlings scrambled to place their own factions on Martian soil. Only, instead of gold, they were hunting technology.

It didn't take long for Martians to rebel. Nationalities were abandoned for factions, and the Overlords seized the opportunity to separate entirely from Earthly control. They were crime lords, and they sold scavenged Martian Technology.

And then, Unity patented the BioMage. More than anything, they realized what the evolved settlers of Mars were capable of. They realized that with the right Earth Tech, they could amplify a BioMage's effect. So, in the year 2990, Earth became one nation.

And Martians became their own.

* * *

"I *told* you that I needed to temper her immediately!" Doctor Ravin held me at arm's length, and I vomited into the proffered bucket.

"Just fucking do it!" Ori shouted over the shuddering, screaming ship.

"Ori!" the com over our heads shrieked, Harry's voice carrying the whip of command. "Help Brute!"

"There isn't time!" Doctor Ravin shouted after Ori.

As the slender woman began swearing, she switched to of-then Russian. She seized my shoulders and thrust me back on a gel-like operating table, securing my wrists at my sides. I started to scream. She shoved something like putty into my mouth.

"One in five people die in accelerated evolution," she growled, switching back to heavily accented English. "One in three die in untempered accelerated evolution. But who cares about the statistics?"

My eyes were wide, my gagging reflex was squelched under putty, and all I could do was follow the doctor with my eyes while she scampered around my table, jabbing buttons and securing me. I tried to pull free, but a brick would have better luck at squirming free of its wall. Doctor Ravin's dark hair was secured in a tight bun at the base of her skull—which did nothing to distract from her giraffe's neck—and strands flew around her sweaty face as she worked.

The ship gave another shuddering jolt, and Doctor Ravin went flying into a table of medical utensils, the clattering tray preluding a string of what I could assume were Russian curses. She whirled to me, eyes wild.

"You'd think that after all of these years," she snarled, pulling a syringe from her pocket, "she'd know how to fly the goddamned ship."

She jabbed the needle into the side of my neck. Something cold filled my veins, and my eyes rolled back in my head. The ship shivered. I shivered. Ice slithered into the dark recesses of my brain.

"Thirty days since the last journalist," she said, even as a cloak of darkness obscured my vision. "He isn't even cold yet, and we're accelerating another corpse into the ground."

A second jab, this time in my wrist. And the doctor's words slowed, deepened, came to my ears as though underwater.

"If—I—had—two—years—like—the—rest—of—the—universe—I—would—never—lose—a—patient—but—no—we..."

Her voice faded into the black.

I wondered if I was dead, and the thought sent my heart racing. It pounded through my body, a cavalry charge. But if I *was* dead, then what exactly was I supposed to do about it? I felt like laughing. Some part of my subconscious obliged. The ship began to vibrate. I think it was the ship, at any rate.

What ship?

"Like a phoenix from its ashes," I had written, "the Firebird rises."

And we shall rise again. Unity bleached the Earth. They controlled us, but only so far as the BioMages were capable of. I remember when my mother discovered that I was a Mute. I remember staring into her eyes, her unnatural, light blue eyes, so alien in her black face. I remember her trying to convert me, having access to the most powerful amplifiers. But she said it was like screaming at a deaf woman. She said that I was unique.

She said that I was broken.

Defective. A Mute, someone who BioMages could not alter, who was deaf to their will. Unity would not suffer the weak. They did not tolerate Mutes any more than they did the mentally unsound. Except that instead of burdening society, I threatened it.

Unity had a singular way of dealing with threats.

"Are you going to turn me in?" I had asked her.

My mother wore the white robes of her office. Her hair, slate grey and cropped short, was greased back. She stared at me. She stood in the center of all she represented, a figure of intellect and Unity authority, and she bared her teeth.

As an Empathetic BioMage, my mother had the ability to read people's minds. And as one of the Thirteen, she had the power to make that perception a truth. Forging my papers was simple for her. Destroying the doctor's mind, the poor man who examined my mental state, had been as easy as falling down.

And somewhere in the simple easiness of her task, my mother was changed.

"She dead?" Ori's voice floated through my brain.

"She should be," Doctor Ravin snarled. "You call that a landing, Harry?"

"Bite me," the crackling voice on the com suggested.

"Where'd we hit, anyway?" Regina's voice.

"Chryse," Harry said, static-lined.

"Well then. We're fucked, aren't we." It wasn't a question.

My eyes snapped open, and I lurched upright, meaning to take a gasp of air. Instead, I found my mouth full of putty. My nose wheezed as I sucked in the oxygen, heart accelerating.

"Easy!" Doctor Ravin shouted, stumbling backwards as I jumped from the surgical table.

Rather than falling to the floor, I launched myself halfway across the room. The table that caught my ribs made the precious air I'd managed to breathe go rushing out again. I hit the floor, eyes watering in pain, and squirmed. I tore at my mouth, trying to get a hold on the putty.

"You're damaging your—" Doctor Ravin started, scrambling toward me.

I punched her. The delicate nose snapped under my knuckles, blood spraying down her face, and she fell back. She fell back hard. And her Russian swearing was squishy behind her hand.

I dug my hand into my mouth, seized the putty, and ripped it out. Vomit followed soon after, and I let it happen. I threw the putty at the doctor, shoved myself to my feet, and seized the first thing that could be construed as a weapon.

"Get *back*," I shouted, brandishing the empty syringe.

Ori laughed, clapping her hands together and eyeing me in delight.

"She did it. She fucking *did* it!" Ori slapped a hand against a console, the speaker whirring to life. "You hear that, ship? Our journalist fucking survived."

"There's a first time for everything," Harry's voice buzzed back.

Ori, still grinning, thrust her fists on her hips. She had changed out of her armor, now wearing a white leotard—laced with wires and little, blinking red lights—with sweat stains between her breasts and under her arms. Her mop of black hair framed her dark face in a halo.

"Stay back," I whispered, hand trembling.

"Take it easy, damn you," the doctor said, looking down at her blood-smeared hand.

"You're going to let me off this ship," I said, clenching my teeth to keep them from clattering together. "And I'm going home. Do you understand me?"

"I think that you're a little confused," Ori said, nodding sympathetically. I wanted to punch that condescending smile off her mouth.

"No, I think that *you* are. Get out of my way," I edged toward the door.

"Sure, sure," she said, still grinning, stepping to the side, hands held mockingly in front of her.

I scowled at her as I rotated, backing from the room, sweat trickling between my shoulder blades. It was too damned hot on this ship. I slapped my hand against the black screen beside the exit and the door whizzed shut with a rush of air. Through its round window, I could see Ori. Her white teeth flashed when she started laughing.

Swallowing panic, I turned to the hallway. It had a rounded ceiling, circular doors dotting its expanse, and when I started running, my feet were too light. The floor was the same, strangely adhesive texture as the operating table, and each step launched me forward. Too quickly, I was at the end.

I tried to stop. The floor gripped my boots as I did so, but my momentum flung me forward. When my face smacked into the wall, it was my right eyebrow that took the bulk of the blow. Stars exploded in front of my eyes. Down the hallway, I could hear Ori laughing.

I rolled to my knees, dropping the syringe. It took me a second. My lungs burned horribly, and though my instincts had me sucking in air, the oxygen hurt me. Pulling myself to my feet, I drew a shaky breath and slapped my hand against the door's latch. There was a second's hesitation, gears whirring within the heavy wall, and then—with a sucking sound—the door snapped open.

Air rushed around me, chilling my damp skin, and I stared at the black membrane. Someone shouted my name down the hallway. I grit my teeth. And I leapt through the door.

The same blackness. The same absence of air. And then, a world.

I screamed as I fell. Or, rather, was vaulted from the ship. My momentum carried me maybe twenty feet, and I hit the ground rolling.

The air was saturated with the heavy scent of soil, like I had just dropped into a greenhouse. Water dampened my clothes as I slid to a stop against the base of a tree. I blinked up at the sky, framed by gigantic leaves, and my brain throbbed.

The sky was a deep shade of purple, stars winking softly through the hazy atmosphere.

I rolled to my knees, coughing. My stomach was a withered raisin, so instead of bile, I heaved up stale air. My dark hair trembled in front of my face, dripping. I could *feel* the humidity condensing on my flesh. I blinked water from my eyes, staring at my dark hands. My veins stood up too far, farther than I'd ever seen them, and the bones in my fingers *hurt*.

"Ever hear of taking it slow?" a woman with a soft, often Australian accent asked.

I pushed my damp hair back, straightening—still on my knees—and narrowed my eyes at the pilot. She climbed down from her ship with practiced ease, and her face sported a small, sympathetic smile. She had hazel eyes. Her dark blonde hair was pulled back in a ponytail. Her sleeveless shirt showcased powerful arms, and the suspenders gave her a strange, ancient-fashioned look.

"Where am I?" I demanded. Or rather, I meant to demand. When I breathed, the humidity stabbed at my lungs. Another coughing fit had me doubled over and weeping.

"Well," the pilot—Harry—said, moving to my side, patting my back softly. "You really should consider it. Adapting is hard enough when done properly. Right now, you're trying to breathe water before your gills are fully grown."

"I'm not breathing water," I gasped, though my lungs burned to the contrary.

"It's the oxygen content," Harry said, sagely. "And nitrogen. It's just different enough. Once you finish adapting, it'll be straight fuel. But until then," a small shrug, "it's a little uncomfortable."

I scrubbed my sleeve across my eyes, blinking at Harry. She wore no makeup, but her skin was smooth and golden. She tucked my hair behind an ear.

"It took me a few months to regulate," she said.

"I don't understand," I wheezed, looking at the purple sky. "Where are we?"

Harry sighed.

"I told them to be gentle," she shook her head. "But the situation deteriorated rapidly. Dragons took out one of our fuel cells," she jerked her chin back toward the ship. "We barely made it, as it is."

I looked at *Redwing*. She did not have the smooth, grey contours of a Unity vessel. Instead, three sets of thin wings stretched out from each of her rust-colored sides. She rested on the soft earth with a spider-like delicacy, long and low. The cockpit rested slightly higher than the rest of the ship, windows black.

"Made it where?" I asked, voice thick.

She grimaced.

"Mars."

6

MARS

"That's not possible," I told her.

Harry nodded, rising slowly, offering me her hand. I hesitated before taking it. Her fingertips were rough.

"It's not," she assured me.

I looked again at the purple sky. We had landed in a little glade, the trees surrounding us were a mixture of thick and short, and tall and thin. The leaves on the shorter ones were as long as I was tall, and half as wide. The tall ones wove drunkenly toward the canopy, limbs twisted. Nothing touched. They had grown with several inches separating every branch, trunk, and leaf. Staring at them made me dizzy. I looked at Harry.

"How long was I out?"

"Better part of three days," she said.

"That's not possible," this time, it was a whisper.

"For Firebird, it is."

I shook my head again. Tears threatened, and I squelched them under a blaze of fury.

"Am I a hostage?" I asked.

"I wouldn't say that," Harry murmured.

"Captive?"

Harry shrugged.

"For now, perhaps. She wanted you, risked her life to get to you."

"Who?"

"Firebird."

I squeezed my eyes shut. When I shook my head, it was firm.

"No. No, I don't believe that. You're saying that *the* Firebird risked her life to get to me? I'm not worth that. I'm just a fucking journalist." I paused, adding sincerity. "I'm no one."

"She apparently thinks differently," Harry met my eye. "Despite our protests, she allowed herself to be captured in your Sector, knowing that you wouldn't be able to pass up the opportunity to interview her."

"*Why?*" I hissed, pulling free of the pilot's formidable grip. "If she wanted me so badly, why not just *ask* me?"

She shrugged again.

"I suppose she was concerned that you would reject her proposal."

"Better to fucking kidnap me?" I snarled.

A smile flickered.

"Betters the odds on you not rejecting her, doesn't it? Besides. For what we need, I think she'd rather have you believed to be dead."

"I don't understand."

"That makes two of us. You're breathing easier," she noted, nodding. "You must have an aptitude for Martian air. We've noticed that people with your African descent have an easier time with—"

"That's the other fucking thing," I cut her off and took a step back. "It takes two goddamned years to get from Earth to Mars. I'm not an idiot. This is some kind of trick. Some kind of simulation."

"Why in the worlds would we go to all the trouble?" She looked like she wanted to laugh, but restrained herself to an ironic smile.

"I don't know. Maybe you want Unity looking for your criminal asses on Mars instead of on Earth. I *know* that Firebird is Earth-based."

"How do you *know* that, exactly?"

"Because," and I threw my hands up, "it takes *two years* to get to Mars. Firebird's raids used to come every couple of weeks. She wouldn't have the resources on *Redwing* to sustain the raids. She'd need a base camp."

Harry sighed.

"You've the patience of a god," someone growled from behind me.

I whirled, hand darting instinctively to the satchel that was no longer at my hip. A woman stepped from the dark cover of the alien forest. She had short hair and wore an old-fashioned cowboy hat, black and pulled low over her eyes. I saw three scars running down her left cheek. Her duster was a dark, mottled leather, and it whispered across the grass as she strode toward me.

More intimidating was the long-barreled rifle she slung over one shoulder: s*niper, Spider variant, powder-based.* I narrowed my eyes at the weapon. It had several mods that I didn't recognize and was nearly as long as she was tall. The woman marched toward me until I was forced to take a step back. She had a mouth that looked like it had never known the stretch of a smile.

"What makes you say that, Rawn?" Harry asked.

The sniper spat toward my bare foot.

"Can't condone a woman who dismisses the evidence of her own eyes," she had a thick Irish brogue, and when I met her eye beneath the brim of her black hat, I saw that one was green, and the other blue.

"This can't be Mars," I repeated, and even I could hear the loss of conviction in my voice.

The sniper growled something, in what I guessed was Gaelic, and strode toward the ship, duster swaying. When she had hauled herself through the door, I asked Harry:

"Was that Rawn Laurensen?"

"The one and only," Harry nodded. "Prickly as the legend itself."

"Not in my legend."

"Maybe that's why Firebird wanted a word," she smiled. "Getting our characters messed up, laying our legends in shallow graves."

"If it weren't for me," and I clenched my fists, "Firebird wouldn't be a legend at all. The only people who would know about her would be the few who witnessed the crash. And they would have been destroyed by Unity."

"Exactly!" Harry clapped me on my shoulder. "You're catching on. Now come on, lend me a hand."

"What?" I stared as the woman moved around me, walking toward the back of her ship.

"A hand, *yar* Lurk. We've got a ship to fix."

I gaped after her. The forest around me was alive with sound, strange bird calls and stranger insects. I could hear a big something moving somewhere to my left, and fear tickled between my shoulder blades. Quickly, I followed Harry.

"I don't know anything about spaceships," I mumbled.

"That's fine. I know enough for the both of us. What I need from you are literally your hands."

"What for?"

"For carrying."

We reached the back end of *Redwing*, and I stopped dead.

"Brute!" Harry said, slapping the figure on the back. "I've brought the muscle."

And, while I hadn't worked out a day in my life, I couldn't argue with her. I certainly wasn't to be known for my intellect at the moment. I stared at Brute, my mouth hanging open.

"Oy!" said the hovering, oversized volleyball, swiveling toward me. "I've been *dying* to meet you!"

"You're Brute," I whispered.

"And you're Lurk!" she said, enthusiasm bringing her already girlish voice to a strained pitch. "Sweet fur on a whirbal, it's a pleasure to meet you!"

A quarter of the robotic volleyball was black glass. Within the glass, I could make out a young woman's face. She was Japanese, hair braided in pigtails, and she grinned at me with open excitement. Her fingers rested lightly on two panels within the sphere, and when they moved, the sphere moved too. Her legs—thin and fragile looking—were crossed on a red velvet cushion. She bowed to me at the waist.

"God," I said, bowing in return.

"Not quite," she said with a wink. "But given time and technology, nothing's impossible!"

"Brute," Harry said, frowning as she touched a blackened gash in *Redwing*'s side.

The girl twitched her fingers and her ball whirled, zipping to Harry.

"Not as bad as it looks," she assured her. "Gonna have to get a new cell from Chryse, but the rest can be repaired with spare parts. Our last expedition left us plenty well off."

Harry shook her head, still frowning at the damage.

"It'll be delicate work," the pilot said, like a surgeon questioning the sharpness of her scalpel.

"Luckily for you," Brute said, whirring back from the damage. "I'm a professional!"

The way Brute spoke brought exclamation marks to my mind: overly enthusiastic. She bobbed around Harry like a puppy learning the word *walk*. I took a step back from the pair. Something squirmed beneath my heel.

"Hell," I flinched, jerking my foot back as I saw a beetle the size of a golf ball wriggle through the grass.

"Oh, there's all kinds of nasties here," Brute said, lowering her voice in mock confidence. "If it weren't for Jiggy, I would never venture from *Redwing*."

"Jiggy," I asked, staring suspiciously after the massive insect.

"Jiggy!" Brute agreed, whirring around me so that she could bob an inch from my nose. She gave the sphere an all-encompassing gesture. "My savior!"

"I've never seen anything like this," I said, leaning back from her. "It's incredibly sophisticated technology."

"Why, thank you!" Brute grinned, swinging her pigtails from side to side. "I designed her myself! Go ahead and say hello, Jiggy."

The sphere's circumference lit up with fast, bright lights. When Brute spoke, the lights brightened and dimmed with her tone.

"Brute is our engineer," Harry said, clapping a hand on my shoulder. "She's the reason we're all alive."

"Oh, gee-whiz, Harry," Brute bobbed back and forth, like a nervous shuffle. "I'm saving my own skin, while I'm at it, you know."

"We're aware," Regina appeared behind Brute, arms crossed.

"Oh, you're always so crabby," Brute told the big woman, her lights shifting to a violet shade. "You don't have to bully the new recruits, you know."

Regina answered with an arched brow, and I was disconcerted by the way her biceps flexed as she tensed. When her beady eyes returned to me, I felt something in the pit of my stomach turn to liquid.

"Firebird wants you," she told me.

7

WRITER

———

Unity valued scientific pursuits. Art and literature were taught only in dark rooms, by people who sometimes disappeared. There was socialized healthcare, education, and food. You had an allotment delivered to your door at the beginning of every week, and it was yours to do with as you pleased. Restaurants and bars were still plentiful, but the people who filled them were generally from the upper crust.

If you weren't a scientist, doctor, or engineer, you didn't make money.

There was no poverty, not in Unity's bleached world. Children began their education at an early age. Middle schools taught of-then high school-level courses. By the time they were fifteen, they had of-then college-level degrees. And when they turned seventeen, they took the Aptitude Test.

There were three fields any Unity citizen could aspire to, and so there were three branches of the test. Everyone took them. When Unity rose in 2990, they'd found me in Oxford. They'd found all of us. And while they disbanded the literary, cultural, and artistic departments, they corralled the students in a long, bleached building. And they gave us our test.

The only reason I was not taken to a small room, laid down in a coffin-sized bed, and had my veins filled with poison is because I passed—marginally—the Medical portion of the test. My mother had been a doctor, you see, and some things stick with you. She'd always wanted me to go into the medical field.

I think it's the reason I became a journalist.

I'd failed—fabulously—in Engineering and Natural Science. Luckily, each score from the three portions was tallied separately, and my general lack of understanding in robots and terraforming was not a prelude to my early demise.

Most of my friends were not so lucky. In fact, when they flew me home at my mother's request, I never saw any of my friends again. And when *Yo* Ruse personally tested my BioMage aptitude, I should have joined them. In truth, I'm still surprised that I didn't.

* * *

"Jezi," Firebird said.

Regina led me into a small, dark room near the center of the ship. The decorations were muted reds, and they took the form of long drapes. It softened the room, as did the disgusting, brown shag carpet under my feet.

Firebird laid on a narrow bed with black sheets, propped up with a couple of block-like pillows. Her bruises were darker in the low light, giving her hawkish face a haunted look. She regarded me with her reptilian eyes, and I felt a spurt of anger.

"I don't know what you're trying to pull," I said, voice higher than I would have liked. "But I'm not going to be a pawn. Why you felt the need to capture the only journalist on

Earth who tries to help you, I have no idea. I had a fucking life, you know."

Firebird listened, unmoving. So, I clenched my fists, took step forward, and continued:

"If you're thinking that you can hold me hostage to influence my mother, you're dead wrong. She'd kill me herself if she thought that it was best for Unity, and she'd kill me if I threatened her position. I've made you a legend, and people love you, but if you're going to hold me captive and feed me lies—just like fucking Unity—then I'd rather stab out my eyes with a goddamned pen."

At last, I got a reaction from her. Just, you know, not the one that I had been expecting.

Firebird smiled.

"And it is that dedication to the truth," she said, soft and low, "that made me realize your potential. You do not hide the facts. You don't spin them to make me or anyone else look good. You uphold a set of values, and your readers can *feel* sincerity when they're reading your work. That's not something easily earned, and it's not something you can learn. You write. And you have the potential to change the worlds."

I glared at her.

"I *did*. But my credibility is shot. Either Unity thinks that I'm dead, or they know that I'm with you. Either way, you've lost me my job. Do you think that my writing just magically appears? I've got to go through channels, channels that I now can't attract attention to, because the people who run them would be found. If they're even still there. After my contact with you, they probably went to ground. You've destroyed my life."

"That's what rebels do," she stated, each word separate and distinct.

A pause.

"Tell me something, Jezi," Firebird folded her hands on her stomach, fingers bandaged. "Why write about me? That first story, the helicopter crash. People died. Innocent people. People in a hospital. Unity proclaimed me a murderer, and the world was inclined to agree with them. What did you see that they did not?"

I continued to scowl. Regina was a hulking apparition at my back, and I could feel her beady eyes on me. I considered turning around and giving the big woman a taste of my knuckles before storming off the ship. But, since I was a head shorter and half her weight, it wasn't likely to have the dramatic effect I was looking for.

"The coronary report," I growled.

Firebird raised an expectant brow.

"The helicopter was a transport for Mutes being sent to the Room. The coronary report didn't include them."

"The official report had them in it, proclaimed dead to the world."

"Yeah, but my mother was a doctor. And she worked at that hospital."

"You're trying to tell me that she shared confidential information with you?"

I snorted.

"My mother wouldn't share a meal with me. But I've never been a good child."

Firebird watched me for an uncomfortable length of time. When she nodded, it was with the solemnity of a decision made.

"You are not a captive, Jezi."

"You sure about that?" I asked. "I was just tied to a table by a woman with all the couth of an eighty-year-old grabbing a nurse's ass. I'm being fed lies, told where to go, and threatened by she-hulk," I jabbed a thumb over my shoulder at Regina, in case there was any doubt.

"My people have not lied to you."

"Bullshit. *You're on Mars?* What kind of idiot do you think I am?"

"The special kind," Regina mumbled.

"You are on Mars, Jezi," Firebird said.

"Bullshit," I repeated.

"I thought you liked her because she was clever?" Regina asked.

"You've met Brute," Firebird said.

"I have," I answered, although her tone hadn't implied a question.

"Then you've met the reason we're alive. Brute is an engineer, and she is armed with Martian technology that Unity has no way of understanding. We're able to out-maneuver them because of that technology and Brute's talent. We know how to jump to Mars in two days, and we know how to get back to Earth in less."

Fear, cold and wicked, squirmed to life within me. I stared at Firebird, and the possibility that she was telling the truth had the strangest effect on my blood. I shivered.

"If you're lying," I whispered, "then to hell with you. And if you're telling the truth, then you've not only destroyed my life, but ripped me away from everything I know. Either way, I won't help you. I fight Unity, but I fight it because it's evil. If you're evil, then I'll fight you too."

Firebird sighed, and her mouth tightened.

"You'll find that the line between good and evil is only an idea made by lesser men. If you are to change the worlds, Jezi, you must first conquer them. And no conqueror has ever been wholly good, nor entirely evil. We are what we must be, and our roles are defined by circumstances we cannot control.

"What I want from you is simple," something in her gaze hardened, and I felt that horrible pressure between my eyes. "Live with us. Fly with us. And, if you desire, abandon us. It is your choice. No one in my party is forced to remain. They are free, and their freedom grants them reason. Do as you wish. Leave, if you must.

"But remember this, Jezi Lurk. When you first gave me my name, when you first defied Unity and wrote my story, you did not do it because of who I did not kill. You didn't even do it because of who I *did* kill. You did it because you want to change the world.

"And here," she closed her eyes, easing back against her pillows, bandaged hands on her stomach, "is your chance."

8

EERIE

"*What* are you wearing?" I stared at her.

Granted, I had bigger problems. But when Ori entered my room wearing an ancient-styled black suit with a bow tie and a bowler hat, I couldn't help but be a little taken aback. Her hair was like a black cloud pluming out from under her hat and when she flashed that white grin, there was mischief in her eyes.

I was coming to expect that.

"You like it?" She asked, hooking her thumbs in her lapels and turning, giving me a look at all the angles. "It's what all the kids are wearing these days."

"You look like you fell out of a history book."

"That's the idea, baby," she made finger guns at me. "You ready?"

"Ready for what?"

"Biggie's Chryse."

"Isn't that a bay of the Circumpolar Ocean?"

Ori looked, in a word, appalled.

"Oh, sugar, *no one* calls it the," and she pushed a pair of imaginary glasses up and adopted an extremely irritating voice, "*Circumpolar Ocean.*"

I gave her as unamused an expression as I could.

"The Ocean Borealis, then?" I asked.

"Jesus, Mary, and Joseph," she rolled her eyes skyward. "Is this what Earthlings are like these days? Gods above, I never knew how lucky I was."

"You're Martian-born?"

"Born and raised," she whipped the bowler off her head, dropping a deep bow. "Ori Ier'Chryse, at your service."

"Ier?"

She gave me a withering look.

"You're joking, right?"

I scowled at her. My room was the same size as Firebird's—all the quarters had seemed of similar shapes and sizes. Mine lacked decorations, and the grey walls were familiar after Unity, but the hammock was piled with pillows and blankets.

"*Ier* means something like *of the sector*," Ori said, after a lengthy silence. "Usually, only the Overlords and their minions bother with it. But I sort of fancy it. Like an introduction to my name."

"I see," and I turned back to her. "So, what do you call the ocean?"

"This part's just the Chryse. It's more than a bay. I mean, it's the size of a sea on its own. Mars is half water, you know."

"I know."

"Well, we've got Chryse. And we've got a few thousand rivers. And then we've got the big fucker."

"Is that what it's called, then? The Big Fucker?"

She stared at me.

"You cracking wise?"

I shrugged.

"I'm not feeling particularly funny."

"Might want to see to that. And let me know when you do. I wouldn't want to forget to, er, slap my knee." She flashed that white grin. "The ocean's divided into three sections, like a big ole pie. You've got our part, the Loch System. And then you've got the one to the west of here, the ole Terra. And the third, well, it's just the Vallis. So, Loch, Terra, Vallis: the Ocean Borealis." She winked. "We learned that in primaries."

I sighed.

"We learned of-then Earth geography."

"And how's that working for ya?" She didn't pause for me to answer. "You ready to go, or what?"

"Go?"

"To town. To Biggie's Chryse!"

"Who's Biggie?"

This time, her jaw dropped. I felt like hitting her.

"Only the Chryse Overlord, sweet cheeks. She's the lady of the century, runs most of Mars and more than you'd think of Unity. And her town is where that new fuel cell is waiting."

I made a noncommittal sound, running a hand down my filthy, red blouse.

"They have transport ships there?"

"I suppose they do. But not ones that an Earthling would do well to be seen coming in on, if you know what I mean."

"I don't."

"Of course, you don't," Ori sighed. "Well, they're the black market of transport ships. If you're looking for a shade more legal, you could hire someone to get you to Phobos. The space station is just a hop, skip, and a jump from there—literally, if you're sporting a suit—and they'll have the Earthbound ships. But if you're being smart about that thing, you'll know that you can't board those bad boys without the proper papers, and honey, you don't have them."

"I used to," I mumbled, shoving my hands in my pockets. "But now I don't even have clean fucking underwear."

Ori shrugged.

"Me neither."

A day on Mars is only thirty minutes longer than one on Earth. And so, when Ori and I emerged from my room—her dressed like a gangster and me like a recently homeless politician—I discovered evening.

Harry and Brute were waiting for us outside of the ship. Brute looked very much the same in Jiggy, except now she wore something bright, pink, and frilly and the lights on the sphere had a rave-like pattern. Harry wore the same suspenders and dark pants, but her shirt was now long-sleeved. Her hair remained in the low ponytail, and the hat she turned over in her hands was a dark fedora. She smiled at me.

"Good to have you along," she said, turning to the forest. "We were starting to wonder if Regina had made good on her promise to carve you up."

"She's insane," I said, matching Harry's stride as we started into the trees.

"Can't argue with that," Harry admitted. "But if I were you, I'd take that crazy in stride. She's a good woman to have on your side in a fight. And a really fucking bad one to have otherwise."

"Duly noted. But I meant that she was insane, if she thought she could take me." Harry glanced at me and I winked. "Pilates."

"Pil-what?" Ori said around a mouthful of fruit.

"Gods," Brute said, her semi-robotic voice deeply disturbed. "Did you just pick that up from the ground?"

"Looked tasty," Ori said, swallowing. "Could be worse."

The sky had turned the color of a fading bruise, and the stars were little more than a suggestion. I could see the two moons, and they were small and fast in comparison to the one I'd grown accustomed to. Within the forest, I could smell nothing but damp, warm soil. I couldn't tell if it was the humidity or my own sweat that had my shirt plastered to my skin, but I felt sticky, dirty, and exhausted.

"I'm surprised the Doctor isn't coming with us," Brute said, whirring ahead of us, little pink sphere bobbing through the thick trees. "She usually won't pass up the opportunity for a heavy drink and saucy dancing."

"The only dancing that twat gets done," Ori said, spitting a seed at Brute, "is with an empty bottle."

"A drunk doctor is better than no doctor at all!" Brute said.

"Well that's just not true," I mumbled, following Harry over a thick, mostly decomposed log. Something large and fat wriggled out from under one of my hands.

We came to a small clearing. At first, all that I saw were two small aircraft. They reminded me of Jiggy, if Jiggy were the size of an SUV. They had the same light patterns rotating around their circumference and their domes were of the black, fracture-proof glass that Unity was so fond of.

"Once she leaves here," a cold, leathery voice said in a heavy brogue, "she'll know enough to get us all killed."

Rawn Laurensen leaned against a thick-bodied tree on the edge of the clearing, her duster tossed back from one hip to reveal a powder-based revolver. The lower half of her face was covered by a dark handkerchief. *Someone*, I thought, *has been watching too many classics.*

"What do you want me to do?" Harry asked. Her tone sharpened, losing the patience that I'd grown accustomed to. Instead of looking at Laurensen, she focused just over her head.

"Well," and the sniper spat as she shoved herself away from the tree, "I'm not going to be here when Unity comes crushing down on us. You remember the last Earthling we adopted?"

Harry stopped so abruptly, Brute bumped into her. I hedged sideways. The pilot was bristling, her shoulders tight and her hands in heavy-veined fists at her sides. Ori glanced at her, then shook her head ever so slightly.

"Shut your fucking mouth," Harry growled, as low and ominous as a lioness moving to protect her cub.

"So, you do remember," Laurensen's eyes glinted over the handkerchief.

Harry took a step toward her, sharp and with violent intention, and the air behind Laurensen *rippled*.

I blinked, my eyes refocusing on the twilit trees. Some...*thing* moved, its hooves crackling on the forest floor. When it snorted, it reminded me of nothing so much as a horse, but the monster lurking at Laurensen's shoulder was *not* a horse. I saw an eye, roughly the size of a baseball, inky, liquid black, and I saw scales. They were rimmed with silver, like dewdrops clinging to the serrated edges of leaves, and of the same dark, glassy nature as the ship's windows. When it lowered its head level to Laurensen's shoulder, I could see small, dark, curling horns sweeping back from its brow.

And when Harry didn't stop, the creature opened a pair of black wings, rose onto its hind hooves, and *screamed*.

"Jesus," I gasped, meaning to take a step away but catching a heel. When my ass hit the soft earth, I scuttled backwards like an inverted crab.

Harry ignored the monster. She stopped in front of Laurensen, nose close to the sniper's. The beast bared its teeth, and they were fat and white within the horse-like face. When it pawed the ground, I felt the earth beneath me tremble.

"You got something to say, might as well say it," Laurensen said, not backing down, eyes as sharp as Harry's.

"You ever mention her, *anything* about her, again," and Harry's voice was as brittle and sharp as shattered glass, "and I'll kill you slowly."

As far as threats go, it was straight forward. And maybe, if it had been said by someone other than Harry, it would have been silly. But, as it was, something in the words made a ring of truth shiver just beneath my flesh.

I pushed myself to my feet. Brute bobbed at my shoulder, lights whirring and anxious, and her little robotic voice found the clearing like a hesitant swimmer touching a toe in an icy pool.

"Harry, we'll be late."

Harry and Laurensen stared at each other for a beat longer. Before turning, the pilot spared a glance for the monster. The beast's neck was arched, wings half-spread, and when it snorted, its breath made the loose hair around the pilot's face quiver.

Harry returned to us in silence. The cockpit of the transporter whipped open when she placed her hand against its side. The machine hovered a foot off the ground, and when prompted by Harry's fingers, the orb rotated forward, dipping the cockpit toward the earth and turning the rim into a step.

"Go on then," she said, nodding at me.

I climbed into the shuttle, careful not to look over my shoulder for fear of antagonizing the monster. The interior of the ship was red, a circle of soft cushions rimming its circumference, and I found a spot as far back from the door as possible. Brute whirred in after me, then Ori. Harry was last. She met Laurensen's eye as the cockpit whipped closed.

"Families," Brute said, settling next to me. "You understand."

For the first time since I'd met her, Ori was silent. Harry took her place in the center of the room, sitting with her legs crossed, a joystick on either side. She took a settling breath. Her back was to me, and I could see that sweat darkened her shirt between her shoulder blades.

"She didn't mean it," Brute offered. "She's just trying to protect us."

"No one," Harry's voice was raw, "understands the risk better than I do."

Brute went still, her lights turning to dark blue, and I felt that she was wise to keep her silence. Harry took three settling breaths. Then, with a gentle clearing of her throat, she flipped the little safety-keys off on the joysticks and the engine beneath us whirred to life.

"This," said Harry, the ship rising from the ground, "is *Galaxy 2*."

"You name all of the ships?" I asked, watching the dark figure of Laurensen dwindle as we took to the sky.

"I didn't," and the sharpness in her voice returned, broken and bleeding.

"But they *are* all named," Brute agreed, lights turning to soft purple. "And quite well, I might add."

I'd read that life on Mars was comparable to an of-then rainforest, but that had always struck me as a poor analogy, since Earthlings hadn't seen a rainforest in over three-hundred years. A better analogy was a greenhouse, for it was sweltering and humid, and life was plentiful.

Harry took us in a slow, vertical ascent, letting the world splay out for me. The floor of the shuttle was glass, as was the rounded belly, so my perspective was that of a being within a bubble, floating hundreds of meters over the ground. The forest had a gentle glow to it, and I remembered someone telling me about the bioluminescence of certain Martian plants. Over us, the sky continued to darken from its purple, pulling us toward endless black.

Blacker than even the sky, was the Mars north of us. I could see where the forest ended and the Ocean began. It was like spilled ink, so vast it seemed unending, and it made something uncomfortable settle within me.

"What was that creature," I asked, forcing my mind from the helplessness of my situation. "The one with Laurensen."

"That's Eerie," Brute said, lights swirling from purple to a burnt shade of red. "She's a Martian Nightmare."

"I'll say," I nodded. "But what is she?"

"A Nightmare," Ori said. "It's what horses evolved into, when they were adapted to Mars."

I let that sink in for a beat.

"Bloody hell," I said.

"Truly," Ori agreed.

"I knew that life evolved differently here," I shook my head. "But I didn't realize it was so drastic. Humans look essentially the same."

"We've had less time here," Harry said, flicking a few buttons on a screen at her side. "When we're adapted, some of us gain telepathic abilities."

"BioMages," I agreed.

"Precisely. And when we first adapted horses, their intelligence increased to the point where we could no longer tame them. They ran wild on Martian soil for a few hundred more years than humans. And Martian air has a way of...accelerating the evolutionary process."

"Just look at me," Ori said, tipping her bowler back. "I'm obviously more evolved than you simple mouth-breathers."

"You don't look anything more than human," I argued, frowning. "But that, that *Nightmare* was a monster."

"She's been around that gun-slinging nut case for too long," Ori said, shaking her head. "Most Nightmares go out of their way to stay out of yours. They're quiet, and won't bother you so long as you stay the hell away from their foals. Eerie is the only beastie that I've ever seen take a rider."

"Laurensen *rides* that thing?" I felt my brows climb.

"From what I've heard," and Ori winked at me, "that's not the only thing she does with it."

"Ori," Harry murmured, twisting one of the joysticks and arcing our flight northward.

"What? You're telling me that you're going to defend her, after that mess? You're a right strange one, Harriot."

"Don't," and the ship suddenly whipped to the side and dropped into a dive that thrust my stomach somewhere into my throat, "ever call me that."

"But it's your—whoooo!"

Ori's argument dissolved into a rollercoaster-level of thrill as Harry whipped the shuttle forward. I grabbed the edge of my cushion as gravity vacated our dome and the world turned to a dark purple blur. The shuttle shifted, twisting my field of vision, and I became abruptly aware of Harry's need for speed.

There was a golden ribbon beneath us, and I would have mistaken it for a strange, yellowish, glowing river had we been moving any slower. Instead, as Harry thrust us into it, I realized that it was a kind of highway. Shuttles similar to ours honked and screeched at Harry's arrival, but she ignored them. Both joysticks were thrust forward and my stomach took a vacation next to my spine, having tired of my throat. Ori continued her manic laughter, Brute giggled within Jiggy—bouncing from the cushion to the ceiling—and I stared, jaw hanging, as the road twisted sharply downward. If the road was a yellow river, then this was a waterfall into a lake of molten gold.

"Welcome," Harry said, a smile in her voice, "to Biggie's Chryse."

9

GREETINGS

A Martian city was like an Earthling city in the same way as a Nightmare was like a horse.

"Every road has four lanes," Harry explained. "You've got incoming and outgoing traffic," she gestured to her own lane, and that opposite. "And you've got the incoming and outgoing autolanes."

These were reddish-hued rivers of traffic that ran on the outer edges of our own and the outgoing lanes. Traffic there moved at a slower, regular pace.

"What's an autolane?" I asked, edging closer to Harry.

"When you enter it, you put your destination into the con," she pointed to the black screen by her knee, "and it autopilots you to it."

"But it's much too safe and slow for our Harry," Ori said, lounging on the red cushions like Athena, a glass of blue wine in her hand.

"Don't see the point in taking all day just to get anywhere," Harry said, somewhat defensively.

If Martian roads were rivers, then Martian buildings made canyons. Colors whirled past us, entire skyscrapers flashing through ads. Music played, and despite the soundproofing within our shuttle, I could feel the bass through the glass floor. Harry twisted the joysticks and we dropped, streaking down a side stream of traffic. The skyway narrowed, and when I looked up, the peaks of the skyscrapers were lost to dizzying heights.

"You look terrified," Ori observed, sipping her wine.

"Earth doesn't use hovercrafts," I said, forcing my eyes from the tops of the buildings. "Oh hell," I continued when my gaze found the ground, which was red and rushing up to greet us.

"Mmm," Ori nodded, popping something square into her mouth and talking around it. "It's a real ball-buster sometimes."

"Martian gravity combined with Martian technology allows for efficient lighter-than-air craft," Brute said.

"Ori," Harry said, shifting the levers and pushing past a slower shuttle.

"Mmm?"

"We've got company."

"Comp—" I started.

There was a flash of violet light, like a firework, and when it hit the back of our shuttle, static shot around the circumference of the sphere. Brute made a high, pained sound, zipping from her place by my shoulder to the center of the globe, lights going cold and blue. Harry swore in a language I'd never heard and Ori grinned.

"It's about time," Ori said, rising from her cushion, white teeth bared as she looked out the back of our shuttle.

Only ten meters behind us, a triangular ship shadowed Harry, sleek and scarlet. To either side of its nose, twin guns glowed purple. Harry angled our descent, zipping between two narrow buildings. A second later, the scarlet ship appeared.

"Beautiful. Here," Ori whipped her bowler off her head, tossing it at me. "Keep track of that, baby. And here," she grabbed my shoulder and hauled me up with shocking strength. "I'm going to need that."

The cushions at the back of the ship lifted, and an array of firearms displayed themselves. The scarlet ship released another shot and Harry twisted the joysticks at the last second, sending us spinning violently to the side. I gasped when I hit the floor, rolling twice over before I rammed against the edge of the pilot seat.

"Woo!" Ori howled, grabbing two red guns. "They're color-coded for efficiency. Blue for electric, green for acid, and violet for plasma."

"She likes colors," Brute said, bobbing in the affirmative.

"Yeah," and, one gun slung over a shoulder and the other tucked into the back of her black suit, Ori tossed back the rest of her wine. "And baby, I like fire."

She threw the glass at the back wall, where it struck a small, orange button. The back end of our shuttle shivered. And then, the dome of glass lifted, opening our ship to the pursuing vessel. Ori jumped onto the rim of the craft, leveled the red gun, and howled as the enemy ship began to recharge the violet guns.

When Ori fired—*Winston automatic, fire-based rifle*— the rifle barked like an old-style powder-based rifle. But when the bullets cracked against the pursing vessel's windshield, they didn't merely shatter the glass. They *exploded.* Ori leaned back, long legs braced against the doorway, and laughed. And she fired until her gun clicked empty.

"BRACE!" Harry shouted.

Ori threw the gun under her arm and grabbed twin handles on either side of our shuttle. A second later, Harry twisted the ship and we whipped to the side, shooting into a tunnel. White lights screamed past us. I found myself on the opposite side of the ship, sliding across the glass like a freshly greased seal, and Brute zipped to my side.

"It helps if you take ahold of the handles," she said, simple as stating that it was easier to breathe through my nose than my ears.

Ori howled again, and I sat up in time to see the enemy shuttle shoot into the tunnel behind us. Another vessel wandered into its path and it blew it out of the sky, twisting upside down to avoid the wreckage.

"What do you need?" Harry shouted over her shoulder.

"Bastard can take a hit!" Ori screamed in return, still grinning.

She pulled the heavy-barreled pistol from her belt— *Winston, fire-based, AKA peashooter*—and braced her wrist with one hand, closed an eye, and began squeezing shots off at the scarlet ship.

"It's a Ridger," I shouted, pushing myself to my knees, arms shaking.

"So?" Harry shouted in return, weaving through traffic like a bat navigating its cave.

"So," shaking or no, I managed to make it to the guns. "Shoot it in its cannons with acid."

I handed the green pistol to Ori, who tossed the peashooter to me. It was scalding hot and when I dropped it, it crackled against the black glass.

"Whatever you say, baby!"

Ori took a breath. The scarlet ship's guns glowed violet. And when she shot the ship's cannon, the violet light flashed white before dissolving with a gurgle of black sludge.

"Yeah, baby!" Ori screamed, squatting and shooting the other cannon before hitting the black windshield with three more rounds.

"You won't be able to melt the glass," I said, shoving a black gun at her. "They reinforced against elements with the Ridger 3000s, but that leaves it brittle. The pilot sits just right of center."

Ori made a sound—something in between intrigued and bored—and took the gun from me. Harry bolted out of the tunnel just as Ori put a bullet through the glass. So, all that I saw of the crash was a streak of scarlet crushing into a land transport and an explosion of green fire.

"Well I'll be damned," Ori said, flopping back into the shuttle and slapping a hand against the orange button. "The journalist is a bloody gun aficionado."

Brute zipped to Ori's side, a fresh glass of blue wine hovering in front of her. Ori tossed the third gun to me, accepting the wine and taking half of it down in a single gulp. When she smiled at me, her teeth were stained.

"Who'd have thought, am I right?" she said, nudging Harry's shoulder with the toe of her combat boot.

"You know not to do that," Harry growled, easing us back onto a skyway.

"I know," Ori crossed her legs. She frowned at me. "Where the hell is my bowler?"

I blinked at her, black gun in my dark hands, and we both looked down to the last place I had fallen. The hat was beside Harry's chair, resembling less of a bowl and much more of a Frisbee. When Brute started laughing, it was high and uncomfortably robotic.

"I've got to hear this," Ori said, frowning at the hat. "How the hell did a little Earthling journalist know how to take down one of Biggie's enforcers?"

My chest tightened. Of course, I'd been waiting for the question, known it was only a matter of time. But still. The lies tangled within me, strangling me from the inside out.

Martian government was simultaneously a miracle and a disaster. Resembling nothing more than a massive system of gangs, they avoided anarchy by a questionable margin of Overlords. That I knew of, there were five. And the Biggie that Ori referred to turned out to be one of them.

Only I knew her as the Overlord Mariana.

The bounty on her head would give the highest officials in Unity pause. She not only killed every Earthling sporting a Unity uniform, she publicly sentenced them to death. Unity had no power here, and Mariana was one of the five reasons why.

I'd studied her. I'd studied all of them. Extensively, and in greater detail than Firebird could have imagined. The problem was, naturally, that I shouldn't have had access to the intel Ori was questioning.

"Unity requires us to study Martian tech," I lied.

"Mmm," Ori gargled the wine, swallowing slowly and giving me a crafty, wicked kind of look. "That's right. They wouldn't have approved of your artsy-fartsy degree, would they? Made a girl switch over to science."

"Yes," I said, flat as day-old beer.

"Well, here's to that," Ori laughed, thrusting a second glass into my hand and cheersing me in the same gesture. "Who'd have thought that Unity's sciencey curriculum would save our asses?"

"Who'd have thought," I agreed, sipping tentatively at the wine. It made me want to choke. From its color, I would have guessed that she was downing Boones Farm. But it tasted like nothing so much as a strong, fresh, pinot noir.

"Arlin's finest," Ori said, reclining on the cushions. Her hair had been pressed flat against the sides of her face from the wind, and I noticed a tear on her left cuff, presumably from where one of the guns had snagged a stray thread. Otherwise, I wouldn't have been able to tell that she'd recently shot down a ship from the back of a flying shuttle.

"You are all insane," I said.

Ori met my eye, her smile widening.

"One of us," she chanted. "One of us."

10

CHRYSE

Some part of me had expected that we were going to Biggie herself. I'd anticipated for it, prepared for it, and when I'd handed Ori her guns, I'd even slipped a spare revolver into the back of my red suit. Just in case.

But what I hadn't expected—what no one in Unity could have expected—was that Firebird was as wanted by Biggie as she was by Unity itself.

Harry put our shuttle down in an alley that was marginally wider than the shuttle. As with the rest of Biggie's Chryse that I had seen, the buildings were unfathomably tall. I stepped out of the aircraft with a strange, tingly sensation in my legs, my eyes traveling up the side of a bright, flashing building.

And, my God, the noise.

First and foremost, there was the music. Speakers were inlaid in the structures throughout the city, and they played strange, smooth, electronic, 1920s-influenced music. It flowed through the building canyons, as soulful and alien as the purple sky I could no longer see.

Secondly, there were the engines. Lighter-than-air crafts zipped overhead, like a few million lightning bugs, and while they were relatively quiet, the sheer volume meant that the air positively thrummed with power. I could feel the static of it pressing against my flesh.

And last, there were people. They were screaming, laughing, singing, whispering, and shouting. They moved with reckless abandon. With so few ground transports, the streets seemed primarily reserved for foot-traffic. Unlike Unity, the Martians were without limitation. They ran, they jumped, they danced in the streets.

All of this, and I felt *small*. I was a bit of flotsam on a river that I hadn't even known was there. I turned slowly, trying to take it in, and only succeeded in making myself feel grossly insufficient.

Harry hopped out of the shuttle after Ori and Brute. She had an old-style revolver tucked into the back of her belt, and she winked at me as she adjusted her fedora low over her hazel eyes.

"Don't try to absorb it all at once," she advised. "The Chryse is the largest city on Mars. It's overwhelming, sometimes even for us. The key is to know what you want, to keep your head down and to get it done."

"Truly," Brute said, whirring over to hover by my ear, "the key to any successful travel is to always know where you're going, where you've been, and where you are."

"Pfff," Ori snorted, unwrapping a candy and popping it into her mouth. "The Chryse is where it's happening, baby," she gave her hips a suggestive wriggle, hands in the air. "If you're going to have a good time on Mars, this should be where it's at."

"Keep your head down," Harry repeated, pulling an oily, heavy-looking bag out of the shuttle and thrusting it into Ori's hands. "And get it done."

"Could let the girl at least get to know the place," Ori grumbled, slinging the bag over a shoulder. "S'all I'm saying."

"Come on," Harry nodded to me, leading us out of the alley. "We've got some errands to run."

We were not, by any means, on a main street in Chryse. And yet, the volume of humanity vibrated in the air. The...*energy* of the place was like an infection. I felt the world moving around me. And, as I hoisted my own bag of heavy, greasy engine parts over a shoulder, I kept my eyes fixed to Harry's back.

People in Unity wore grey. Maybe black, and occasionally white, but mostly, they wore all the shades of grey. Colors were unnecessary. Color resided in the things scientists studied and had no place on the scientists themselves. It had cultivated its own sort of subculture, where journalists and other unessential members of humanity were shamed into wearing red.

My own red blouse—filthy as it was—felt cleaner than it had in years.

Because here, no one spared my shirt a second glance. There were no condescending smiles, no coy jokes about how writing was as fruitful as flipping burgers. Because here, the only color that I didn't see was Unity grey.

Here, people wore their reds as badges of courage.

And they *danced.* An entire section of street was being blocked off by about a hundred people swing dancing. There were women dressed as of-then *flappers.* And there were women dressed as gangsters, not unlike Ori in her black suit and bowler. Some of the men wore suits, but the vast majority wore some kind of retro renovation of a 1990s disco.

I'd never seen such a mess, and it made a hidden part of me laugh.

"What's going on?" I asked Harry's back. "Why're they celebrating?"

"Do they need a *why*?" Ori asked, punching my shoulder, flashing her wide grin at the people around us. "It's another night and we're alive."

"So, it's *always* like this?" I shook my head, gaze sweeping up the impossible buildings to the sky I could not see. "I don't know if I could handle it."

"You can, and you will," she elbowed me, skipping a few steps in time with the, frankly, catchy music. "No one can be on Mars for long without becoming at least a little Martian."

"Don't freak her out," Brute rebuked, zipping to Harry's shoulder and floating backwards, watching us. "It's only her first night. She hasn't even gotten over her jumplag."

Ori made a disgusted face.

"I thought we'd agreed that you wouldn't call it that."

"What do you want me to call it?" Brute swiveled back and forth, lights flashing yellow. "Jetlag isn't dramatic enough for a two-day jump from Earth to Mars. She's on a different planet."

"It's the same thing," Ori shrugged. "Just, you know, *better*."

"Simmer," Harry said, stopping outside of a building with a neon sign of a martini glass tipped to one side. "We've got work to do."

"*We've got work to do*," Ori repeated, her voice in a mockingly low imitation of Harry's Australian accent.

"Hey, that's really pretty good," Brute said, lights flurrying to pink.

Harry gave her a flat look from under the black fedora. She sighed.

"Piss off. Jezi," she turned to me, something like a smile softening her face. "We've got to pick up a crewmember in here. You should know, Martian drinks carry a bit more of a kick than Earth's."

"Jesus, Harry," Ori said, shouldering past her. "Are you going to start breast feeding her, next?"

The pilot stared at me, her expression flat, before shaking her head and following her crewmember into the bar. I glanced at Brute. She bumped Jiggy against my cheek before shepherding me after them.

The bar was jazzy. The lights were low, the wood was dark, and the bar top was a clear plastic that was lit from beneath. It gave the already ghostly-pale bartenders an ethereal look. Ten or twenty tables sat around a small dance floor, which was in front of a stage. A tall woman sang soft and smooth up there, her male accompaniment playing something that looked like a cross between a saxophone and a trumpet. It just had too many fingerholes.

"See her?" Harry asked Brute, her eyes narrowed.

I coughed. The room was hazy with pipe smoke, and it seemed to glitter in the air, like a dusting of powder gold. Ori was at the bar, one of her rifles propped carelessly against her thigh, and she had two drinks in front of her. She turned, caught sight of me, and beckoned me over.

"Damn girl," she said, throwing an arm around me as I reached her. "You smell like a dead cat."

"Why a cat?" I asked, eyeing one of the drinks she pushed toward me.

"Jezi," she said on a sigh, "Do you have to question everything?"

"Whatever gave you that idea?"

Ori stared at me for a second, then said in the least amused voice possible, "Clever."

She shook her head, picked up the glass, and downed it. I looked again at mine. It was in a tall martini glass, and I couldn't tell what color it was for the smoke that was rolling off the surface. I looked again at Ori.

"It's called an Olympus," she said, smacking her lips. "And it's better than your momma's kisses."

I made a face at her, but took a sip of the drink. It was so cold, I felt my tongue go immediately numb. But she wasn't wrong. It was sweet and smooth, something like pineapple.

"See," she slapped my back, turning me to face the room. "Good things happen when you listen to Ori."

"How long have you been referring to yourself in the third person?"

"The third what?"

I shook my head. Harry and Brute had moved to the far side of the room, where a woman in the corner leaned over a short drink. A red, wide-brimmed sunhat hid her face. Harry pulled out a chair and took a seat across from her, only to be ignored. Ori squeezed my shoulder.

"Finish that up. We might need to lend a hand."

"I don't understand," I said, taking a slow sip—it really was quite good. "Isn't she a crewmember? Or are you kidnapping her as well?"

"Hell, honey, you've got some sass in you. We didn't kidnap you—we rescued you. Unity would have turned your ass over the coals if they thought even for a second that you'd had unrestricted access to Firebird. Hell, a BioMage like that could make an Overlord turn a gun at her own throat. No, baby. We pulled you out of hell. And if you'd hurry up with that baby bottle, we'll go over and try to do the same for poor *Yar* Okeke."

I frowned, but did as I was told. Something cold clicked against my teeth at the bottom and I gasped, spitting and sputtering. My lips burned where it had touched them.

"Jesus, Jezi, didn't your momma teach you not to eat dry ice? Come on," Ori grinned, taking my glass and slapping it down on the bar. "You've got more friends to make."

She kicked the rifle up and into her hand before leading me away from the bar. The room was tight and the tables were close together, and I navigated them with the slow, careful steps of an old woman. My head felt light, my stomach felt cold, and I was grossly aware that I couldn't remember the last time I'd eaten. When we stopped at Harry and Margaret's table, I sat without being offered a chair. The world seemed a little too tipsy to trust standing on.

"Who's this, then?" I asked, squinting at the top of the red sun hat. "A member of the Red Hat Society?"

"Isn't that the old lady—" Brute started, lights whirling to light pink as she giggled.

Harry gave her a look. And then she gave me a bit of one as well.

"Margaret," she said to the hat. "We've got a journalist."

The hat's brim lifted, and I angled my head, trying to get a peek at the contents. I saw two hands, one on a short glass of dark liquor, and the other on a snub-nosed pistol. It was pointed at no one in particular, but the gesture seemed less than inviting.

A pair of dark eyes caught mine, and the quirk of a smile within the folds of the hat's shadow was strangely white.

"Did you, now?" she asked, her accent of-then African—*Nigerian.*

"We did," Harry assured her, her hands folded on the table. "And we're going to need you."

"Everyone needs Margaret," she said, snorting. "But who's paying?"

"What's with people and the third person?" I asked, looking from Ori to this Margaret Okeke character. "I can't feel my face, but you don't see me talking shit about how Jezi can't feel her fucking face, do you? And I'm the bloody writer.

So, if anyone is going to be taking liberties, it's by God going to be Jezi."

"Jezi," the hat's brim angled, cutting Harry out of the equation and giving me a full view of the woman's face. "Heaven help us," she said, leaning back from the table. "You got her."

"We did," Harry said.

"Got me?" I asked, both brows arched.

Margaret was a dark-skinned woman in her late fifties. She wore her hair in neat pleats, nestled snugly to her skull under the red hat, and her lips were painted white. She wore a loose-fitting, sleeveless dress and turned her whiskey with short fingers. When she smiled, it was somehow ironic.

"Whatever they're paying you," she told me, "it is not enough."

"I don't know that they're paying me anything, yet," I confided, head feeling warm and light, stomach feeling cold and iron-filled.

She shook her head.

"Sugar, she's doing just fine without—" Ori started.

"No one is talking to you," Margaret said, not looking at her. "The muscle is for flexing, not for speaking."

"Godfuckingdamnit," Ori snarled, gesturing sharply at Harry. "I *told* you that she'd do this. She's not worth it."

Harry raised her hand, and Ori snarled something before marching back to the bar, shouldering several people out of the way in the process. Harry met Margaret's eye for a solid minute. When she leaned forward, I felt myself involuntarily drawn in.

"We've found the coordinates for a payload," she said, voice low.

"Oh, have you now," Margaret gave her a smug smile. "And how have you managed that, exactly?"

"Brute," Harry said, still low, still leaning forward.

Margaret looked at the hovering robot for the first time. I found myself wondering how someone could possibly ignore such a thing. I blinked, shaking my head, trying to clear it. The colors in the room seemed to blur. The woman's face softened.

"You've been keeping yourself busy then?" she asked, her tone turning motherly instead of the chilly interrogator the rest of us had been subjected to.

"That last payload," Brute said, whirring closer to Margaret. "It was something of a double-edged sword. You know the thing we found, the thing that...well, the *thing*?"

"I do," Margaret cocked a brow.

"Well, after the smoke cleared, and I had some time to study it, it turns out that it was...well, it *was*."

Margaret swirled her glass, watching Brute. When she drained it, I noticed that her eyes didn't leave her. She sighed.

"It was what was promised?"

Jiggy's lights whirled to yellow.

"It was."

Margaret looked to Harry, but nodded toward me.

"And with a proper journalist..."

"We could take back the world," Harry nodded, her hands tight in her lap. "But we need your help."

"Of course, you do. And the Lord's too, thought it does not need to be said." Margaret sighed again, and I saw the glint from an of-then Christian cross against her chest.

The room began to spin. I frowned, unsure if I had laid my head on the table, or if it had fallen there. But the last thing that I heard before the world turned into a dark, humming madness, was:

"Alright, Harry. But I have one condition."

11

REDWING

"*Sermons,*" Ori hissed, the sound of something shattering coming soon after. "You're going to let that witch-hunter *preach* to us?"

"I'm not going to *let* her do anything," Harry snarled, and her patience sounded raw. "She's free to preach and you're free to ignore it."

"Except that you've given her an hour on your goddamned intercom. There won't be a village on Mars that won't be subjected to her caterwauling."

"Then wear headphones, Ori. You know that we need her."

Ori apparently didn't have a good argument against that, because the only sound that followed were the retreating footsteps of her heavy boots.

I opened my eyes to find myself in my room on *Redwing*. My hammock was swaying gently, and it was that gentleness that made me throw myself from it. I barely had time to find a bucket before my insides were convulsing and bile erupted from me.

"I told you to go easy on that," Harry said, sliding my compartment door open.

I didn't answer, merely continued emptying myself of the meager contents. When I finished, I shoved the bucket as far from myself as possible, sprawled on the floor and met Harry's eye.

"What happened?"

"Ori carried you back," she shrugged, leaning against the doorway. "We got what we'd gone for and cleared out. Biggie's not pleased."

"You could say that again," I rolled to my knees, expecting my head to start throbbing.

"How do you feel?"

"Actually," I said, rising slowly. "Not that bad."

Harry nodded.

"The adaption assists biological recovery," she smiled. "You heal quickly."

I shook my head, suddenly, violently hungry. My quarters were as barren as ever. Harry, noticing my glance, beckoned for me to follow her.

"Come on, then. I'll show you the kitchen."

Harry led me down the hallway lined with doors. She nodded at a few, empty now, pointing out the biology lab— which doubled as Doctor Ravin's experimentation room—and the areology lab, where Margaret's red hat laid on a table full of dusty instruments. We passed a crossway of corridors, cockpit to the right, engineering to the left.

"Feel free to roam the ship," Harry told me, taking the left corridor. "If you want to talk, we're usually at our stations or in our quarters. And, to be fair, if we're in our quarters, we're probably sleeping."

"Just a spaceship full of workaholics?"

"You could say that," Harry pointed at a room with a circular port for a door. "Brute lives in the computer science lab."

"Imagine that. You know, I haven't agreed to do this yet."

"I know."

"But you told Margaret that you had a journalist."

"Sure," Harry glanced at me over her shoulder, smile crooking the corner of her mouth. "But I let her surmise which of us it was."

"Is she some kind of fan of mine, then?"

"I wouldn't go so far as to say *fan*. Margaret is a woman of God. Everyone she meets is second-best *at* best."

"Strange," I said, as we stepped into a room near the back of the ship.

"Why?"

"On Earth, all religions have been bleached out. You don't really meet fanatics anymore. Unless they're Unity fanatics, that is."

Harry didn't answer. The kitchen was a slightly larger room, painted a dark shade of red with a light blue table and mismatched chairs. Ori stood behind a long counter, steam rising around her face and making her plume of hair stand on end. She flashed her smile at me.

"Hungry, pumpkin?"

"Starving," I said, glancing at the ceiling, where a surprisingly delicate mural of a rose had been painted.

"Well, hold onto something," Ori said, plating a heap of what looked like scrambled eggs. "Because I'm as fine a cook as you'd ever want to meet."

Harry exchanged a look with me that left me with my doubts, but all that she said was:

"I'll let you refuel. When you're feeling up to it, come on up to the cockpit. I'm going to get us in the air."

I watched Harry leave while I took a seat at the table. Ori slammed the eggs down in front of me, looking plenty pleased with herself, and I had to admit that they smelled amazing. Of course, in my state, I would have drooled over roadkill.

"You like?" She asked, watching me eat with the rapt attention of a hawk.

"Spicy," I gasped, searching for water.

"You Earthlings," she laughed slapping my back with an enthusiasm that made me doubt her innocence. "Never could handle some fire. Here," and she thrust a thermos into my hands. "Cool off, wimp."

I chugged. It was flat, like water that had been sitting on a counter for a few days, but I didn't mind. I wouldn't have been surprised if my mouth began to steam.

"Damn girl, you stink. I'm going to go find some fresh clothes for you."

"Thank you," I said, around another mouthful of the damning eggs. "Don't suppose that there's a shower in this place?"

"There is, but you can't use it," she winked at me. "Not while we're in the air. Take a sponge bath like the rest of us mortals. See you, wimp."

"That's not," I started, but Ori was already gone. "Okay."

I finished my breakfast and searched for a place to wash the plate. Ori had left the kitchen a right disaster, and I stared at it for a minute in utter horror. I'm a neat sort of person, and while there didn't seem to be a system to where the spices and pans were kept, I made a mental note to have one by the end of the day.

I washed the dishes as best I could with only the thermos of water and a strange, soap-like gel that jiggled in a bowl by the sink. *Redwing*'s engines thrummed to life and I felt the gravity shift strangely as Harry got us in the air. I was just about to wander back to my own quarters when a scream shot down the corridor.

Taking the thermos with me, I darted out of the kitchen. The hallway was empty, and the heat coming from engineering made sweat instantly pop along my brow. The scream came again, high and alien, and I followed it toward the engines, glancing back up the hallway to see if anyone else had noticed.

They hadn't.

At the back of the ship, there were three doorways. The one to the left was closed and, if the red light blinking on the touchpad indicated anything, locked. The one at the back was open, revealing a strange, spider-like engine. And the door to the right was open, twice the size of the others, and literally steaming.

The scream came again and I hurried through, thermos raised like a baseball bat. The steam was so thick, I had to scrub the back of my arm across my eyes. I could feel the water condensing in my lungs as I breathed, and when a black shape surged forward from the back of the room, my shout turned into a choking fit and I tripped.

When my ass hit the floor, the thermos went flying. And so, unarmed and on my back, I watched the Nightmare step forward, head lowered and flat teeth bared.

"Fuck me," I breathed, raising a hand in a futile gesture of protection.

Water glistened along the edges of the creature's scales. It put its nose so close to mine, I could smell its surprisingly horse-like breath. The horns were twisted and black, but its ears were furry and its lashes long. When it nudged my hand with the rough, scaled nose, I flinched.

"Hello," I began lamely, my throat thick with the damp. "Please don't eat me."

The Nightmare's hooves were cloven in the front and horse-like in the back. Its tail was broad and flat, more like a rudder, and when it stomped one of those front hooves, it was so close to my shoulder that it caught the edge of my red shirt and ripped a neat hole. It pressed its nose against my abdomen, breathing deeply. Then, with a toss of its head—the mane was about six inches long and protruded straight from its neck, rubberlike—it lifted its nose and screamed again, eyes rolling down to watch me as it did.

"Living dangerously, are we?"

The Nightmare and I looked at the doorway. Its ears perked up, but I felt myself instinctively shrink back as Rawn Laurensen stepped into the room. She'd ditched the sniper rifle and the duster, but the black handkerchief remained tied around her neck and the revolver rested heavy on one hip.

"I'm sorry," I started, watching the Nightmare as I pushed myself to my feet. "I heard a scream and I didn't realize that...that this was here."

Laurensen didn't answer. She cocked a brow as I rose, gaze wandering from me to the Nightmare. I glanced at the beast, mindful of its ears and tail. I offered a shaking hand and, after a cursory sniff, the creature became bored with me. It snorted and returned to the far side of the room, where it appeared to be enjoying the steaming vents along the edge.

"I spent some time around horses when I was a girl," I explained to the room in general, since Laurensen and the Nightmare were content with ignoring me. "My friend worked on a ranch and I liked to lend a hand, in between classes."

"Didn't ask," Laurensen said, striding to the Nightmare.

"True," I stooped and picked up my thermos. "I'll just go, then."

Laurensen didn't answer until I was nearly out the door.

"You mind yourself. I see you nosing through anything you shouldn't be, and there won't be enough of you to bury."

I gave her a disgruntled glance, but the sniper was focused on rubbing down the Nightmare's wings. When I left the room, I was saturated. I found my way back to my room without managing to get myself into any more trouble.

A fresh shirt and a pair of brown pants were folded on my hammock, my satchel lay beside them, as well as a note that read:

You puked in your sponge bath.

12

AREOLOGISTS

"You look alive!" Brute said, accompanying me to the cockpit.

"I feel less dead," I acknowledged, tucking my loose white shirt into the pants. "These fit pretty well, actually."

She didn't answer, whirring along at my side like one of the personal robot companions that the kids were so fond of on Earth. When I ducked into the cockpit, I found a world whirling past us. The all-glass room gave me the feeling that I was flying, and as I approached Harry's chair, the tingling sensation in my legs climbed—once again—to my ass.

"Woah," I said.

It was midday, by the sun, and the sky was a light shade of purple. Patches of voluminous, white clouds shed a vortex of shadows on the ground far beneath us. We were moving at a fair speed, and I was mesmerized by the dance between light, shade, forests, and rivers. Whereas most of Earth had been either blacktopped or marked as a designated O2 center, Mars was a jungle. I saw flocks of strange, massive birds move beneath us, following *Redwing* with surprising speed before they twisted and shot down a river canyon.

Harry glanced at me, eyes lingering on my shirt. She frowned, and I saw her grip on the joystick tighten. Then, with a deep breath, she glanced up to meet my eye.

"Feeling better?"

"Much," I said, noticing her frown. "Everything okay?"

"Fine," she said, eyes flashing to Brute before returning to her flight. "We'll be arriving at the coordinates in less than an hour. Is Margaret ready?"

"As ready as she can be," Brute assured her, roaming from one side of the cockpit to the other, lights a gentle shade of blue.

"What's at the coordinates?" I asked, dropping down on the floor beside Harry, watching Mars zoom between my feet.

"You remember that we're able to stay ahead of Unity because of our Martian technology?"

"I do."

"Well, you know where Martian Tech comes from, then?"

"Sure. Archaeologists—I mean, areologists—uncover it from ancient sites along the Martian surface. It's how we discovered the terraforming technology that allowed for us to alter the Martian atmosphere to sustain life."

"Right. But all the sites haven't been discovered. In fact, if Margaret is right, then we've not even scratched the surface."

"So, we're hunting down the ancient civilizations looking for technology?"

"Tech, and anything else we can get our hands on," Harry adjusted one of the levers and we began a gradual descent. "Tech is currency on Mars. It's how we pay for fuel. And, if we're lucky, it's how we stay a step ahead of Unity. So long as we find the tech first, we not only don't have to pay for it, but we can sell the parts that aren't a threat. *We* decide how much Unity and the Overlords get to understand."

"And you got the coordinates for a new site from the last one, I gathered?"

Harry paused.

"In a way."

There was something in her voice, something raw and aching, and I didn't press her. I folded my hands, wrapping my arms around my knees, and sighed.

"What a week."

Harry didn't answer.

When we landed, it was on the edge of a cliff at the rim of the forest. Harry put us down as gently as a mother laying her newborn in its crib. The ship came alive with voices, arguments and orders flying along the narrow corridor in a chaotic sort of system. Regina cornered me on my way back to my quarters.

"Put these on," she said, thrusting a pair of heavy boots into my hands. "And don't even think about asking for a weapon."

"Wasn't planning on it," I said, grimacing at the mud-caked boots.

When I got back to this ship, I was going to clean it from cockpit to engines, Nightmare or no. I put the boots on, balancing against the corridor wall and trying to stay out of the way—which was impossible. Regina knocked me over with what looked like a cannon, her square face splitting with a grin when she glanced over her shoulder to see me rising from the ship's floor. I scowled at her, then scuttled backwards to avoid being crushed under the Nightmare, who Laurensen had decided needed to vacate the ship at that exact moment.

I adjusted my satchel, squared my shoulders, and marched off the ship.

Martian gravity took what little grace I'd been given and turned even that against me. My foot didn't seem to come down fast enough, and so when I stumbled, I flailed in slow motion. Margaret, having followed me off, stepped neatly around me and adjusted her hat against the midday sun.

"Blimey," Harry muttered, offering me her hand. "Turn your boots on."

"What?" I blinked at the mud-caked disasters.

She sighed, squatting down and pulling a belt knife free. She chipped enough shit away to flip a little black switch near my ankle. The boots immediately suctioned against my feet, like little pillow-lined vacuums, and when I raised a foot, there was resistance.

"You'll get better traction," she told me, rising. "And if you play nice, Regina will give you a booster."

"What's a booster?" I asked, watching Harry clip a little receiver to my collar.

"Like a jetpack, but smaller and for your boots," Harry stood, cocking an eyebrow at me. "Otherwise, you'll need to climb."

She left me to begin sorting through the growing pile of rope, rusty tools, and a few, dented electronics that someone was tossing from the ship. I turned, taking a slow, steady breath, the Martian air charging my lungs. I walked to the edge of the cliff.

There was a river down there, and the opposite cliff was some fifty meters away, leaving a narrow canyon to divide the lush landscape. My hands balled into fists, and my feet tingled when I realized that the reliability of anything Regina gave me would be questionable, and the boots were no exception. I eased my balance backwards.

It was maybe two-hundred meters deep, and the rock was sheer, so perfect it almost seemed manmade. There were thick vines growing up its expanse, bright red flowers setting contrast to the dark earth. I could see flocks of birds flying far below me, and every now and then, the black line of the river was disrupted with a white spray.

Something bumped against my shoulder and I froze, my eyes turning in my skull. When the outline of something large and dark took form in my peripherals, I did as quick a sidestep as you've ever seen, whirling to find the Nightmare standing behind me. Its neck was arched, ears forward, and when it snorted, a mist of Nightmare snot cooled my face.

"Careful," Laurensen said, stopping alongside the beast and slapping a hand against its shoulder. "Eerie and I wouldn't want any accidents on your first day."

I gave her a flat look. She had the sniper rifle slung across her back, black hat low and smile malevolent. I nodded at the gun.

"You don't see many powder-based rifles these days. Spider variant, right?"

Her eyes narrowed, and the smile was less of a taunt and more of a suggestion.

"I heard about your little show on the shuttle," she said, spitting over the cliff. "Can't think of any reason a writer should know so much about weapons."

"I write for Unity and spend my free time telling stories about a rebel BioMage and her heavily armed cult. Is it really so hard to believe that I know something about guns?"

"No harder than it is to believe you're a Unity spy."

I paused. Then, I stepped smoothly forward. Laurensen was tall, but I wasn't very short myself, so when I put my nose close to hers, I could look right into her dead, mismatched eyes.

"If I was, you'd be dead already," I said, simple and without emotion.

She stared at me. And then, the corner of her mouth quirked toward a grin.

"Perfect," she said.

Laurensen shouldered me out of the way, stepped to the edge of the cliff, turned her back to it and spread her arms wide.

"Just know this, Lurk. People tend to betray me, and I like to make sure they don't die with the first shot."

And she tipped backwards.

Despite my suctioned boots and distance from the edge, I still felt my heart give a nasty lurch as the woman threw herself from the cliff. Eerie tossed its head and charged forward, wings spreading as it surged into the air. The rudder-like tail fanned open, revealing silver membranes between the black, scaled bones. It turned and shot down the canyon's gullet, screaming its ethereal war cry. When Laurensen pulled herself onto its back, the two angled sideways and shot up the canyon.

"Son of a bitch," I whispered, scrubbing a sweaty palm against my thigh.

"Oy, Lurk," Regina called. "Get your useless ass over here."

We unloaded the rest of the equipment—I arranged it as neatly as the others had the patience for—and when we were finished, a diverse array of equipment was scattered across the soft, Martian soil. Margaret cocked her head, one finger tapping against her white lips. The red hat's floppy brim twitched as the wind picked up. She clucked her tongue.

"Right, then."

That didn't seem like much of a command to me, but the crew immediately set to putting on climbing harnesses. I grabbed the least worn-looking one, stepping smoothly into the straps and tightening them with quiet efficiency. Harry checked my work, seeming surprised.

"Do much climbing back on Earth?"

"Not really," I said, watching as Regina clipped the separate lines to hooks along *Redwing*'s side. "But I saw a documentary on it once."

Harry's brows rose.

"You saw a documentary once?" I pretended not to hear the frank disbelief in her voice.

"Eidetic memory," I said, for what felt like the millionth time in my life. I tapped the side of my head. "Couldn't forget something, even if I wanted to."

"I don't know if I could handle that," she murmured, clipping the rope to her harness.

"What about a belayer?" I asked, following her example.

"No need," she gave the rope a solid tug.

It had looked like an old-style, slightly worn climbing rope. But when Harry jerked it, it seemed to shrink on itself, snapping taut against the ship. I followed her example, and my own rope snapped tight, jerking me forward a step.

"Hell, Regina," Harry said, shooting a look at her.

"What?" she glanced from Harry to me, an ugly little smile on her lips.

"*Yeah*, what?" I stared at Harry.

She sighed.

"That one's a little outdated. Let's call it, rusty."

"That sounds safe," I muttered sarcastically, leaning back against the rope. It took quite a bit of pressure before letting me shift backwards, and then it was with an unsettling jerk.

"Works fine," Regina said, clipping into her own.

"Everything works fine until it breaks," Harry mumbled, although I noticed she didn't offer to exchange.

Margaret was the last to clip in. She handed us each a fair amount of gear, clipping it to our belts with a methodical quickness. All said, the group seemed strangely efficient, despite the amount of arguing between Margaret and Ori—

who was sitting on the edge of the ship's wing, eating something like an apple and resting her arms on the shotgun in her lap.

"Y'all come back now, ya here?" she called as we backed toward the cliff's edge.

"We're looking for a site approximately halfway down," Margaret said.

She wore a little, black screen strapped to her forearm like a greave, and she tapped it a few times before continuing:

"The opening will be wide and short, just tall enough for us to walk in. Supposing that it hasn't caved in in the past million years or so," she sniffed. "Probably ought to take it slow."

And with that, we were off. The rest of the group moved in something like unison, repelling over the cliff's edge with sharp, practiced kicks. I followed soon after, gripping my rope and pushing hard. It seemed to stretch, and I could hear some kind of mechanic within it grinding. When I first went over the edge, it let me drop an unsettling five feet before catching again. I slammed forward, feet braced against the cliff's face. My hands were shaking, I could feel my heart trying to crawl up my throat, and I knew that if I glanced down, all would be lost.

So, instead, I focused on kicking from the rock, dropping a few feet, and then catching myself against the cliff's face with the gravity boots.

"Don't forget to breathe," Ori's face appeared over the edge, mouth full.

I looked up at her, caught some apple bits in the face, and drew a deep breath. She hadn't been wrong. My hands quit shaking.

"Move your ass!" Regina shouted from beneath me.

I glanced instinctively down. The crew was a good twenty meters ahead of me. And, of course, as I watched them bob ever farther down, it gave me a strange perspective of how *high* we were.

"Oh, Jesus," I breathed, heart accelerating.

The rest of my descent centered around my hands, because that was what I had to stare at to keep moving. The rock in front of me was a dark shade of red, like sandstone in texture, and the vines were as thick as my thigh and covered in tiny, silvery hairs. I did my best not to touch them.

My legs began to hurt, and part of me wished that Harry hadn't turned the boots on. I shoved myself away from the cliff one last time, thighs throbbing, and found myself suddenly in between Harry and Margaret. Margaret was frowning at her electronic greave, but Harry offered me a solid pat on the back.

"Not bad," she said, drawing a deep breath. "Nothing like getting the blood flowing in the morning."

"Not the kind of blood flow that I prefer," Regina grunted, glowering at the rock's face. "Where the hell is this high-tech cave?"

"We're standing against it," Margaret mumbled, scowling at the screen, turning it this way and that. "It should be here."

"All that I see is a whole lot more rock here," Regina pulled a heavy-barreled pistol from her belt holster. "Want me to see if there's anything behind it?"

"I prefer for my legs to remain intact," Margaret gave her a sharp look from beneath the red hat's brim.

"Could your calculations have been off?" Harry asked, holding a hand up to silence Regina.

"They're Brute's calculations," Margaret said. "What do you think?"

Regina mumbled a few curses, flexing against her rope so that she was essentially perpendicular to the cliff. She laced her fingers behind her head and said:

"I'll just be waiting here, then."

Eerie's scream rattled down the canyon, and I turned to see the Nightmare flying toward us, Laurensen low against its back.

"See anything?" Harry called as they neared.

The Nightmare swept past us, close enough that the wind of its massive wings set us to swaying on the ropes, and as Laurensen brought it back around, she shouted:

"Whole nest of Avies up that way."

Regina snorted.

"This is a good day," her sarcasm had the finesse of an arthritic fencer.

"Avies?" I asked Harry, who watched Margaret begin to poke at the rock wall between the net of vines.

"They're what happened to the pelicans they introduced, back in the 2500s," Harry's mouth twisted. "If you can't find it, we should regroup at the ship," she told Margaret.

"The technical term is Avelaras," the areologist said, not looking away from her arm.

"Well, thank God we cleared that up," Regina said, swinging herself idly back and forth.

Margaret's eyes flashed to the woman.

"Blasphemy will not—" she started.

My rope suddenly released. No warning, no small feeling of dismay. It simply released. With a lurch in the pit of my stomach like a trout hooked in a river, I dropped. I yelped, snatched at the rope, jerking violently and trying to get it to reengage.

It didn't.

I heard Harry shout after me, but my ears weren't working properly. I let go of the rope as I gathered momentum, grabbing the nearest thing—a vine.

As I had guessed, the tiny hairs were sharp, and they dug into my hand as I slid to a stop. Blood began running down my arms, but the pain was second to the adrenaline. I clung to the side of the cliff, bile roiling in my gut. My muscles quivered, and I kicked at the cliff's face, searching for purchase. When I found it, I wedged myself between two thick vines, staring as my useless rope continued to uncoil down from my belt. When it reached its full length—the loop dangling well over halfway to the river below—it swung there like a hanged man.

"*Don't forget to breath*," came Ori's voice through a burst of static on my shoulder, the little receiver blinking.

I sucked in the Martian air. My anger rose as I did so, and a brief fantasy of shooting Regina in the ass flashed through my mind. With a muttered oath, I squirmed between the two vines, arms pressed to the rock's face, blood sticky against it.

And then, something strange happened.

Really, strange isn't the right word. Rain while the sun is shining is strange. Seeing dead people is strange, and being abducted and taken to Mars is stranger. But as my blood touched the smooth rock, red shot up and down the rock in a beam.

At first, I had the irrational fear that the cliff was somehow sucking the blood from my body. But, as I clung there—because I sure as shit wasn't going to shove myself away—the red beam began to glow, warming like a lightbulb. And as it warmed, the light veined out across the cliff. There was a cracking sound, a vibration under my feet.

And then, the vines spread. Truly, it was like someone was drawing a pair of curtains back from the center of a stage—a center that I was standing on. The ledge I'd found with my toes was in truth a piece of metal, and as the vines were drawn away, I found myself standing at the mouth of a metallic cavern.

Little pieces of rock scattered down around me, but not as much as I would have thought would come from a curtain of cliff. I stood, slightly hunched with my arms drawn defensively against my chest, and gaped. The wash of air was cool and alien, a little like earth and a lot like metal. The room was deep, wide and short, and its gullet disappeared into darkness.

The crew shouted at me from above, but I couldn't see them past the folds of curtain. So, feeling the drop at my heels, I stepped into the cave, my boots thudding too heavily against the smooth, immaculate floor. I glanced back, grimacing at the trail of dry clay I left in my wake.

I stood there for a moment, staring into blackness. Then, with a shrug, I squatted down and pressed my bloody hand to the floor of the cavern.

13

TECH

"They would have you killed," my mother had said. "You should be grateful."

As a rule, any time my mother thought that I should be grateful, I was of a wildly different opinion. But this time, all that I could do was stare at her and feel my eyes begin to burn. I remember the way the light played across her dark face. I remember the creases in her forehead, where the amplifier had rested.

Hell, I remember that I had had two cups of coffee that morning, one black and one with cream and sugar—my dessert cup.

There was bitter betrayal in my heart. There was panic building in my extremities, a need for either fight or flight taking root. And, largest of all, there was a sense of wonder.

How could this have happened?

* * *

Strangely, the same wonder found me as I crouched there, bloody light shooting out from my hand. It ran up the walls, down the length of the floor, across and over the ceiling. It filled the Martian cave with red light, both illuminating and warming.

And, with a resounding *bang*, the cliff curtain slammed behind me.

I didn't scream when it happened. Rationally, it was to be expected. If a key unlocked a door, it could only be assumed that the same key would lock it again.

I stood slowly, taking even breaths. Air continued to move around me. I nodded, looking at my hands.

They were raw beneath the blood, like freshly burned flesh. I sighed, lifting the flap of my satchel and digging gently through it. I found the ointment and bandages— although my tablet was long gone. The blisters were only beginning to form on my palms, and when the cool salve made contact, they receded.

The receiver on my shoulder coughed static. Harry's voice was nearly unintelligible. I finished taping my hands before I turned and walked to the curtain, angling my shoulder and adjusting the receiver's frequency.

"*Are you alright,*" she asked me.

"Peachy," I said, dropping my ointment and bandages back into the satchel.

"*Ask her if she can get the damned door open again,*" Regina snarled in the background.

"I don't know," I said, turning to the room, eyes lingering on the equipment.

The lie settled in the chamber slowly, like a ball of dust recently flushed from beneath a sofa. With methodical slowness, I untied the rope from my belt. Then, I walked slowly to one wall, moving up its length, taking in the tech.

"*We're trying to activate it from out here,*" Harry said. "*Try to stay calm.*"

"Doing my best," I said, quickening my pace.

"What happened the first time it opened?"

I let them assume I couldn't hear them.

The cavern was the approximate length of a football field. There were grids on the floor, like the network of a motherboard, and the ceiling reflected it. Dark glass made the walls, and the lights within them shifted through shapes, lines, and what I could only assume were Martian numerals. They looked strangely familiar. I lapped the room twice.

Then, I walked to its center, sat down, crossed my legs, and waited.

"Lurk," Harry's voice continued, static rattling through the nearly empty room. *"Can you read me."*

I adjusted the frequency to a point where I could vaguely distinguish her words. Then, I said:

"Barely."

"Keep calm. We're trying to—"

I lost the rest of it. I undid the bandage from one hand, loosening it and—in general—ruining it. I pulled the salve from my satchel, spilled some on myself, and then dropped the bottle. A pause. Then, I pressed my elbow against the floor, where my blood had begun to dry, and the red lights flared along the curtain. By the time it had started to slowly grind open, I was on my back, gasping for air and sobbing.

My brother had always said that I was too smart for my own good. Of course, we had been children, I had not understood why learning came so easily to me, and neither one of us cared about the worlds. Truth be told, he was afraid of me. There was no sibling rivalry. I was six years his younger, and I was an overlord.

When Harry found me, I was a useless heap of sobbing terror. She tried to tend to my injuries and I fought her, screaming incoherently about the darkness. Regina said something about useless people.

Margaret took down information with a scanner. Harry helped me bandage my hands as I calmed and when she was finished, I mumbled a series of garbled apologies, telling her that I was claustrophobic. When I stood, Regina shoved me back down.

"Keep your eyes to yourself," she told me, crossing her hulkish arms.

I shuddered and nodded and let the women do their work.

"Magnificent," Margaret said a few times. "Absolutely incredible."

When they'd collected their data, Harry clipped me into her belt with her safety line. She had the booster mods for her boots, but the weight of both of us slowed her ascent and we had to take several breaks. We both bumped against the vines, and when her arms began to bleed, she didn't swear or cry out. She merely continued her work. And I hung at her belt like the dead weight I was.

Redwing and Ori greeted us at the top of the cliff. She told me that she was surprised to see me in one piece. I didn't answer. When Harry recommended I see Doctor Ravin, I made adequate protests before being shepherded into the ship. She tended to my wounds, swearing quite a lot, and when I left her, I went to my quarters for a lie down.

And lie down I did. I listened to the ship around me. I listened to my own breathing, counted my own heartbeats, and when I heard the world settle as the last of the crew stepped outside, I rose from the hammock and made my way to the computer lab.

Brute was there, whirring happily among the electronics, Jiggy's lights a pale sort of yellow. When she saw me, she exclaimed her happiness that I was alive and gave me a robotic hug that left us both a bit uncomfortable. She explained that she used narrowed gravitational fields as levitation devices—or, as she said, Jiggy's hands—and while I'm sure they were efficient, when she hugged me it was like being squeezed in an invisible vice.

I told her about the vines, about the blisters. I told her that I couldn't get the door of my locker to open because of them. And when she told me that she'd be happy to help, I asked if I could rest for a bit in her lab.

When Brute left to fix my locker, I knew that I had three minutes.

One for her to get to my quarters and fail to open the locker. One for her to figure out that the latch had been broken. And one for her to break into the locker before returning to me. The computer put my back to the door.

My hands were lightning. The computer screens were black, but as my fingers danced over them with passkeys, they showed me their electronic underbelly. It took a minute and a half.

Then, I began to sketch. It was not exact, and that bothered me more than anything had in a very long time, but the idea was there. Martian numerals came easily to my fingertips. The shapes came next. And, as my mental countdown dwindled, I began to trace the lines.

It was crude. I hesitated, frowning, shifting my memory, pushing it onto the screen over my drawing: *thirty seconds.* There was something missing. I squeezed my eyes shut: *twenty seconds.*

My eyes snapped open, and I dragged my finger along the screen, sending it with the final passkey. I slapped an aching palm down on the console, sat back in the chair, and breathed for the first time in sixty seconds. I sensed more than heard the doorway fill, and I swiveled in the chair.

Instead of Brute, when I looked up at the doorway, I was staring at Firebird.

14

ASSIGNMENT

───────

When my brother turned eighteen, he joined Unity.

I remember attending his graduation. He was dressed in the slate grey of a recruit, and when they swore him in, he held his hand toward the earth in a statuesque salute. I hugged him afterwards, and it was like hugging someone I'd never met.

There was a time when my brother and I enjoyed each other, I suppose. He was good at inventing games, I was good at maintaining rules. All things, particularly children's games, require consistency. If there are no limitations, then there is nothing to push. If there is no push, there is no competition, and without competition, the world would not have evolved. Humanity would not exist.

Such a core to our understanding of the universe is inherent, even in a child's imagination. My brother and I could not make these games separately. I lacked the creativity to build a world, and he lacked the discipline to maintain it. It was a characteristic that pursued us well into adulthood. If not for our mother, he would not have risen through Unity. And if not for him, I would never have written anything except the weekly science column in Truth.

He climbed the ranks quickly. My mother said that she had nothing to do with it. She was lying, of course, but he appreciated the tact. When he made captain on his third year, he was put in charge of the Aptitude testing.

Specifically, the Aptitude testing for Sector X.

* * *

"I would like for you to prepare a documentary," Firebird said, stepping into the computer lab, her reptilian eyes on me.

"I've been thinking about my first article," I said, swallowing the ball of panic and proffering a look of innocence. "It's taking me longer than I'd expected. Some of your crewmembers are...less than forthcoming."

Her eyes wandered the black screens behind me. When she looked at me, I felt the pressure between my brows. I had come to recognize it, after the long hours I spent with my mother.

"*BioMages,*" she had said, frustrated, "*cannot control their power. Their will is like a fire. Emotion enhances it, but even a controlled BioMage will subconsciously subject her will during a conversation. You do the same, hoping that a discussion will lean one way or the other. The only difference is that BioMages can change it.*"

"They do not trust you," Firebird said, her gaze lingering on my hands.

"I've noticed," I sighed. "I've done nothing to betray their trust. Something must have happened."

"Must it have?" she stopped in front of a second chair, but she did not sit. She stared down at me. The gentle hum of the computers filled the room.

"It's understandable that they would be wary of a newcomer, given that you'd all be destroyed if Unity found you," I acquiesced. "But their open dislike can only have been inspired by someone else—since I've barely gotten to know them."

Firebird regarded me for another cool moment. Then, she pulled air slowly into her lungs. It was a gesture more significant than merely *breathing.* I got the sensation that I was looking at a snake, its red tongue testing the air. When she spoke, it was a blade bared.

"I recommend that you spend time with each crewmember individually. Assist them in their duties. By the week's end, an article should be prepared. We will proceed to Earth for publication."

"I don't understand why this is so important to you," I said, tugging fitfully at a sore finger. "If all that you wanted was a documentation of your crew, I feel like they could write their own bibliographies with better accuracy than I."

"We're seeking an outsider's approach," and when Firebird smiled, it inspired something akin to terror. "And your name carries weight."

Firebird left me to the computer lab, and Brute returned shortly thereafter, confessing to having broken my locker. She said that she'd figure out a better locking system. I told her that it wasn't her fault. And when I left the lab, Jiggy's lights were a dark shade of blue.

The crew had set up a kind of archaeological camp outside of *Redwing.* Ori and Regina sat on one of the wings, playing some kind of old fashioned card game. Margaret was hunched over a long table, picking at pieces of the cavern that they had extracted. I paused, scanning the camp until I spied Doctor Ravin.

As I approached the woman, I toyed with the strap of my satchel. There were threads coming loose there, and as I tugged at one, I wondered how the doctor could stand the heat. She wore a black suit, dark hair greased back and pale face turned toward the sun. Her nose was delicate, and when I glanced at her fingers, I saw that they were the long, spidery digits of a musician.

"How long since you last played?" I asked her, my shadow throwing her face into darkness.

The little woman blinked at me from her place on a blanket, spidery limbs stretched out as though sun bathing. Of course, I didn't understand the point, being that her only exposed flesh was that of her face. She stared at me, uncomprehending.

"The violin," I said, nodding to her hands. "Or was it the cello?"

"Viola," she corrected, brow drawing. "How did you—"

"Calluses," I dropped to the ground beside her—light flared across her face—and threw on my most disarming smile. "I felt them, when you were...medicating me."

"Impressive," she mumbled, closing her eyes.

"I play the guitar, a little," I continued. "I'm going to miss it."

"I'm certain that a woman of such means could endeavor to procure one for herself, should she ask the right people."

I snorted.

"You mean like Ori? Or—God help me—Regina? Something tells me that these are not women of the artistic nature."

The doctor nodded, hardly seeming aware that she was doing so. I saw faint scars around her collar, almost like a long-healed burn wound. My eyes darted again to her hands, but they were smooth.

"Indeed. One shudders to imagine them at the opera."

I opened my satchel, procuring a small, silver disc. There were a limitless array of vessels capable of storing electronic data, of course, but I'd always preferred a physical copy. The Sky—as Unity had dubbed it—seemed less and less reliable, depending on how private you intended to keep your information.

"I recorded this," I said, offering it to her, "at the last concert I attended. The sound leaves something to be desired, as we gathered in the basement of an abandoned warehouse, but the orchestra was superb."

As though I had slapped her, the doctor's eyes snapped open. She stared at the object in my hand, desire and envy and more than a little despair sharpening the already startling shade of green. She glanced from the disc to my face and back again. She licked her lips.

"I know that Mars has orchestras," I said, shrugging. "But I imagine their music is heavily influenced by the modern tastes. There's a rumor on Earth that the Martian Overlords won't tolerate unoriginal performances. Now I don't know about you, but I have a taste for the classics.

Beethoven, in particular. There's a cool science to it—I'm surprised that Unity banned it, to be honest."

"You heard correctly," she pushed herself up, legs stretched out, and the fingers of her right hand tightened. "Martian musicians are bestial. I have not listened to Beethoven in..." she trailed off, eyes finally moving from the disc and back to me. "I couldn't possibly repay you."

"Consider it a gesture," I said, placing the disc on her knee. "I haven't had the best luck in making friends here. And I could really use one."

"Honesty," she murmured, plucking the disc from her knee and slipping it into a pocket, "and a flair for music. You are wearing at my defenses, *Yo* Lurkshire."

"Please," and I shuddered dramatically, "I would truly prefer Lurk. Or *Yin* Lurk, if it appeals to you. But I'm far from your *Yo*."

"I would hardly consider you *Yin*." The doctor ran her hands down her suit's front.

"You're too kind," and when I smiled, the doctor reflected it. "And if we are to be undecided, I'd like for you to call me Jezi. Unity's prefixes might have seemed logical at the time, but I've never seen the point in putting so much emphasis on politics between friends."

Unity proffered the prefixes *Yo, Yar,* and *Yin* late in their second rise to power. At the time, it was well received, as it offered a sexless alternative to the age-old *Mr, Mrs,* and *Ms* argument. Why should single women be marked as such, whereas single men are still only *men.*

However, as time passed, bias began to build around the *Yo* system as well. Eventually, the structure evolved into a declaration of status as well as a mark of deference (or grounds for slight). I would refer to a superior as *Yo*, an equal as *Yar*, and an inferior as *Yin*.

"And you may call me Doctor Ravin," she stared at me, serious as cancer. "That is nonnegotiable."

Doctor Ravin spoke very little of her home. In fact, if my interview nudged her toward a personal question, she sidestepped it as smoothly as a fencer in a duel. What I did learn, was that she had studied:

"Every form of human adaptation imaginable. We are all unique, and Martian evolution affects us on a molecular level." She shivered, grinning like a girl who'd gotten exactly what she wanted for Christmas. "It's riveting."

"What about me?" I asked, quirking a brow.

"What about you?"

"As a Mute—do I...*evolve* differently?"

"My dear," she patted my hand. "You haven't evolved. You've *adapted*. It's quite different. Like a person who moves from a cold environment to a warm one. They'll wear fewer clothes and they'll tan. Your body would not be able to survive the Martian environment without that adaptation. Picture someone with an inability to cope with heat. They wouldn't tan, they wouldn't sweat, and they would eventually—without modern assistance—perish. The same is true for adapting to Mars.

"But consider evolution," and she leaned forward, her hands moving as she spoke. "A tribe travels from a cold environment to a hot one. Decades pass. Centuries. They adapt to their environment, and their evolution adapts to their adaptations," she slapped her hands together. "And before you know it, they're a new race!"

"But evolution on Mars is accelerated," I said, nodding toward the Nightmare as Laurensen flew toward camp.

"Indeed," she tapped a temple. "The question was, and remains, *why*. People like *Yar* Margaret Okeke believe that all of the answers lie in Martian technology," she snorted, jerking her chin toward Margaret. "But that is like saying Earth's populous evolves slowly because of computers. It doesn't work that way."

"What do you believe, then?"

"Ah," and she thrust a finger skyward, like a detective about to reveal the culprit. "You're skipping ahead. It has taken decades for me to unravel the finer threads of Martian evolutionary theory, and it will take longer for you to extract them from me than the duration of a single interview. You see, my dear, there are—*what in the hell?!*"

Eerie the Nightmare landed in the middle of camp, knocking Margaret's meticulous table over and scattering priceless Martian relics. Rawn Laurensen sat atop its bare, scaled back, one hand against her shoulder, hat pulled low over her eyes. Margaret began to scream at her, accent slurring so heavily that I could no longer tell if she was speaking English. Ori and Regina's card game had gone flying with the wind from Eerie's wings and when they started shouting, it was at one another:

"You *know* that I had the fucking hand!" Ori grabbed Regina by the collar.

"The fuck you did!" Regina retaliated by seizing Ori by either side of her belt and throwing her from *Redwing*.

Doctor Ravin and I stood, and while I stared at Laurensen, the doctor began swearing at Eerie. The great beast tossed its head, and I saw blood the color of ink leak from the scales near its shoulder. My eyes rose to Laurensen.

"Murders," she wheezed.

When she fell, it was toward me. Her hat came off, dark brown hair cut short and soaked with sweat, and blood was sprayed along her jaw. Her hand gripped at a wound on her shoulder, and red pumped eagerly through her fingers.

"Oh, *shit*," I said, turning to the doctor. "Help her!"

Her eyes were wide, her mouth hung open, and that was when I learned the most important thing about Doctor Ravin.

"Blood," she whispered.

And she fainted.

15

MURDERS

"Will someone *fucking help me*?" I screamed over the chaos, blood oozing between my fingers.

Rawn Laurensen lay at my knees, too still for my liking, and her shoulder had been cleanly sliced down to her bared collarbone. When I looked for the doctor, I found her where I'd left her, sprawled senseless on the ground.

"Murders," Laurensen croaked again, grabbing my arm.

"Someone attacked you," I said, looking frantically toward where I'd seen Ori and Regina fall.

"*No*," she hissed. "*Murders*."

"Someone else was killed?" I frowned at her, trying to understand, trying to keep her from bleeding out under my fucking hands.

There came a scream.

No, not a scream. There came a *screaming*. It started at the base of the canyon, rolling up toward us with the distant slowness of a goddamned tidal wave. I turned, staring at the canyon's mouth. The air *vibrated* with the screams.

"Ohhhhh hell no!" Ori appeared from around the ship's wing, tripping over her own feet as she gaped at the canyon. "Oh, no no no."

"What is—!" I began.

The murders rose from the canyon's mouth like a belch from *hell.*

They were the size of pelicans, and their wings were twice as wide. They had the same graceful, curled necks of pelicans in flight. However, when these massive, white birds shot over my head, I saw that their beaks were serrated, their eyes were the size of my fists, and when they dove at us, their talons extended like an eagle's.

I flung myself to the side, over Laurensen, and one of the creatures hit the soil like a bomb, dirt and rocks flying as shrapnel. I covered my face with my arms, rolled once, and pushed myself to my knees.

The sun was obliterated. There were a hundred of the things in the sky, circling upwards like a cyclone, their cries reminding me of a rusty door swinging on its hinges. I spun, tangled in my satchel, and managed to free myself just before another beast dove at me.

Eerie tossed its head, ears laid flat, and when it shrieked, it added a cry of defiance to the cacophony. The beast reared, wings spread, and foam sprayed from its mouth. Laurensen was crouching, one hand on her shoulder, the other held as a shield for her eyes. She twisted, saw me, and her eyes widened.

That was when the creature hit me. I felt the weight of it, like a cannonball, crack between my shoulders. I heard my spine pop, even as I flew forward, even as the ground came up to greet me. The creature was still on top, and when its serrated beak came down, I knew that I did not want to be under it.

With a snarl, I twisted violently to the side, elbowing the creature just under its wing. I felt something crack. Its talons were sharp, and it drew blood as it struggled with me. I managed to get onto my back, heaving at the beast, trying to throw it from me.

Regina appeared behind it, her pale face streaked with purplish blood, and when she snarled, I saw that a front tooth had been knocked free. She hit the creature in the side of its monstrous head with a branch as big around as my waist.

She thrust a hand down to me, and I took it, trying to snatch at a scrap of metal by my boot to use as a weapon.

"What *are these*?" I screamed over the noise, slashing at another creature.

"Avies," she snapped, pushing me behind her as she fended another of the creatures off. "Murders of fucking Avies."

I saw Doctor Ravin scrambling backwards, kicking at an Avie that had taken an interest in her foot. It snapped at her, gigantic wings spread wide, and when she screamed, I saw blood darken her shin.

"We've got to get—" Regina started.

An Avie dove at us. Even as Regina brought her branch around, I knew that it wouldn't be enough. When the bird collided with her, Regina went flying backwards.

And I was behind Regina.

My feet caught against the doctor, and the three of us went over the cliff. It happened so easily, I could scarcely believe it. Even as we picked up momentum, it was surreal. It was like waking up one morning to find your husband gone, with a note on your pillow to tell you that he never loved you. It was as simple and unpleasant as realizing you're a fool.

The doctor was screaming. I was falling a little farther from them, and as I gathered momentum, I was able to angle my descent. I saw Regina snatch the back of the doctor's belt. She looked at me. Our eyes locked, some ten meters separating us. Her hair was wild and blonde, streaking up from her skull, and her baggy clothes crackled.

"I can't lift us all," she shouted.

And she engaged the gravity boots. She did not lurch to a halt, but her descent slowed to a point that I quickly lost sight of her. The bottom dropped out of my stomach and I turned again, spinning slightly. The river, once a hair-wide thread of black, was rushing up toward me, widening at an alarming rate.

There is a moment's hesitation in any freefall. We used to go cliff jumping at an old quarry near my childhood home. I remember the first time, just after I'd worked up the courage to take the plunge. There's a second—an eternity—when there is only air, and time, and the *wait*. There's time to think that this was ridiculous. There's time to realize what a bad decision you've made.

It's the reason people keep jumping.

This was no fifteen-meter cliff jump. I was freefalling, perhaps a kilometer down the canyon, and I didn't have a moment to consider what a fool I'd been. I had a goddamned *lifetime*.

When something grabbed the back of my shirt, I did scream. First, I thought it was an Avie—and wouldn't that be just fucking perfect? Not only would I be crushed to death, I'd be partially eaten first.

But when I struggled, there was an oath. The thing released my shirt and I twisted. If things had been surreal before, they were quickly escalating to the impossible.

Eerie glided in the dive, its rudder-like tail fanned out behind it. Laurensen balanced on its back, her chest close to the wings and her knees pressed tight just behind the shoulders. She was reaching for me. When Eerie's dive trajected closer to me, I managed to snag Laurensen's hand.

"GODDAMNIT!" She screamed, a note of helplessness withering my hopes.

She heaved me onto Eerie. There was no ceremony to it, no coordination or grace. I flailed, thrown half across Laurensen's lap and half across one of the Nightmare's wings. We began to spin, and the momentum nearly threw me free again. Laurensen continued to swear. I could feel the muscles in Eerie's wings *vibrate*. Even as it tried to slow our fall, our dive slipped farther and farther from control.

In the spinning, chaotic, blood-misted world, I had one last second to see the sky. It was black with murders. And then, Eerie's wings caught the air.

Just a moment before we all three plunged into the river.

16

SNIPER

"Her physical abilities leave something to be desired," the doctor had said, leaning back from me.

"But her mental prowess more than makes up for it," my mother's voice was cool and stark, the same voice she'd used when I brought home a questionable grade.

"Perhaps," he sighed. "But Unity is interested in more than just Mutes. We require—"

"She is perfect," when the fourth figure entered the room, my blood ran cold.

I could not tell this person's sex. It was perhaps seven feet tall, as thin as a pencil, and moved with alien grace. Its head was shaved, revealing metal implants along its skull, and when it stopped before me, I stared into a reptile's eyes. The mouth was thin, and it curled when it looked at me.

"You may feel some discomfort," it told me.

And it thrust its power of will against my own. I'd known pain. I'd known more pain than any woman my age had a right to. I'd known loss and heartache, anguish and despair.

There is no pain like the will of a BioMage.

It found nothing, of course. I was a Mute, and all their mental screaming could not render me capable of a BioMage's speech. When it was satisfied, my nose and ears were bleeding, *and I was laying on the floor, blinking tears from my red-filled eyes.*

"She is perfect," the BioMage repeated, the smile pulling back to reveal straight, white teeth.

* * *

Something slammed against my back and I gasped.

Or rather, I would have gasped, but the world around me was a roar and the air that should have been there was water.

I opened my eyes to a special kind of hell. It was gloomy, with purplish light. I was underwater, crushed against a rocky spire, and when I twisted, I could not find the sky. I panicked. I tried to shove myself from the rock, but the force of the current had me wedged there.

I kicked, found purchase on a crack in the spire, and pushed myself away. My foot slipped. And I was spinning.

The world turned white. I had a moment to register that I was surrounded by swirling, gurgling bubbles. And then, emptiness.

The waterfall was horrible. I wasn't thinking clearly. I saw sky and rock and trees spin around me. Then, water. I was thrown deep, and I felt myself beginning to turn in the empty darkness, my lungs heavy and useless.

I don't remember what happened next, except for my satchel's strap going tight and a coldness against my face.

When air was forced into my lungs, I meant to scream for the pain of it. Instead, I vomited. Water erupted from my mouth, burned out my nose, and sent me to a coughing, shuddering, worthless pile of flesh on the riverbank. Tears fled my eyes. I was trembling. And when I couldn't bear to hold myself upright, I fell to the moist ground and gasped for air.

It was there. It hurt me, but it was there. I sucked it greedily in.

For a long while, that was where I remained. Even rolling onto my back required more effort that I had left to give. So instead, I breathed and I waited and I hated the world for hurting me so.

Finally, I managed a sitting position. My legs were sprawled out in front of me, and when I pushed myself to my knees, something in my back ached. I scrubbed a hand against my eyes, blinking.

I was on the very edge of the river, boots nearly in the purple-tinted water. Heavy, green trees burdened the valley, so thick and winding they cast us into an unsettled darkness. My eyes climbed the cliff's wall, but the top was something I could only guess at. The waterfall was a thundering roar, and the swirling black pool in front of me had twisting plumes of foam crusting its surface.

I stood, slowly and carefully, stretching limbs with exaggerated care. Nothing seemed to be broken. I turned, narrowing my eyes at the perpetual dark of the forest.

There were three divots like mine in the soft soil, and my gaze followed them away from the river and into the trees. The trail was obvious, broken leaves and deep, gouged hoofprints. I walked carefully down the beaten path, not trusting the thick, furry leaves.

I found Laurensen and Eerie in a small clearing. The sniper perched on a red boulder, and she was tightening her shoulder's bandage with her teeth. Her hat lay just to the side, on top of the rifle.

Eerie lay tucked around the boulder, and its head popped up when it saw me, ears flat. Laurensen paused in her personal first aid, but she did not look toward me. She merely shifted on the rock and continued her work. Eerie relaxed, head easing back down.

"What," I croaked, my voice grating and lifeless, "happened?"

Laurensen finished with her bandage before she stretched her legs out, toes resting lightly on Eerie's back. When she looked at me, I had the unsettling feeling that she was gauging the distance between us. I glanced involuntarily at the rifle, and was certain that she wouldn't need it to kill me.

"Murders," she grunted.

"I got that part," I shook my head, approaching them softly, a hand held out to the Nightmare. "But what were they? Why'd they attack us? And where are we?"

"You're asking the wrong questions," she grunted, stepping from the boulder and around Eerie.

I frowned at her. Then, gritting my teeth, I shrugged.

"How're we getting back to the ship, then?"

She looked at me, and it was like she'd done it for the first time. She regarded me slowly. And then, she nodded.

"They had coordinates for a drop," she told me, stuffing her hat onto her head. "If we beat them there, we'll regroup."

"And if we don't?" I asked, watching as Eerie shoved itself to its feet.

"Then I'm going my way," she shouldered her rifle. "After I kill you."

I gaped at her, but Laurensen was already moving, Eerie following her toward the river. I hesitated, then scrambled after them, tripping several times over root snarls and rocks. When I caught them, I kept my distance from Eerie's rear end. The last thing that I needed was a horse hoof in my gut.

"You'll kill me?"

Laurensen didn't turn when she talked, and I struggled to hear her over my own breathing.

"I'll kill you."

"Why?"

"Why do you think?"

We came to the river, and Laurensen turned away from the waterfall, walking downstream. There was no trail, but the brush stayed a few meters back from the water and it made for relatively easy walking. I sighed.

"Because I know too much about Firebird, and if you're going your own way, you're going to make damned sure that I don't rat her out."

"Me," Laurensen corrected. "I'm going to make sure that you don't rat *me* out. And after I'm done with that, my contract with Firebird will be severed."

"I wouldn't do that," I muttered, tripping again.

"I don't know that. What I *do* know is that a bullet," she slapped a palm against the rifle, "is a sure thing. I don't believe in taking unnecessary risks."

"That's fair, considering. But are you like this will all new recruits? I mean, there has to be a point when people like Ori or Regina decide that it isn't worth the effort."

Laurensen paused. At first, I thought that she was giving her answer careful consideration. But then, she stopped altogether, and Eerie's ears rotated backwards, its breath hot and steamy in the already muggy air.

I knew better than to ask, and so I settled for listening. The Martian forest was alive with sound. Birds in the canopy, the growling river, the very earth under our feet: the world seemed to breathe. Laurensen turned.

"Earthlings are one and the same," she told me, gaze fixing to mine. "I don't like you, I don't trust you, and if Firebird hadn't entrusted me with your safety, I wouldn't be talking to you now. You'd be drowned, still turning in that pool. So, listen up," she leaned forward. "You do what I tell you. Until we make it to Madtown, you're safe. You're under my protection, as per my contract. If I say to jump, you jump. The Martian jungle isn't something that a wet-behind-the-ears *recruit*," and she put a nasty spin on the word, "should survive. So back up slowly."

"You want me to—"

"Back up slowly," she cut me off, brows raised.

I stared at her as I did so. The ground beneath my feet gave under my boots. Something made the hair on the back of my neck raise. I stared hard at Laurensen as I moved, waiting for her to just fucking shoot me.

Instead, she put her hand on Eerie's nose and pushed it backwards. The Nightmare bulked, not unlike its Earthling cousin, but it obeyed. Laurensen watched the beast's hooves. Or, perhaps, what they getting tangled in.

"What is that?" I could feel my pulse in my throat, slow and steady.

She held up a finger, head cocked. Eerie's legs were covered with thick, sticky white threads. I took another step backwards, and my own ankle snagged against one. They were stretched through the underbrush, like tripwires. And that was when I heard it. It was quick and light, a feather's tapping.

"You know what that sounds like," I breathed, throat tight.

Laurensen gestured sharply at me, her eyes venomous, and I followed her gaze as it moved toward the canopy.

At first, it was difficult to distinguish. The limbs and leaves were so tangled, I couldn't see the afternoon sky. But as I watched, the smallest movement caught my attention. I widened my eyes.

"Is that," I started, not really meaning to speak out loud.

The branches, which had been moving ever so slightly in a hollow breeze, froze. I saw a long, black leg—maybe ten meters, extended—resting against the lower branch. I followed it up with my eyes, guts chilling as I did so.

My mouth was hanging open, and I didn't notice until my tongue went dry.

Laurensen moved with methodical slowness. She pulled the rifle from her shoulder, cocking it with a hand on the barrel, keeping the sound small and steady. Her eyes never left the branches, nor the monster they contained.

The spider's body was hidden mostly in shadow. The giveaway was the dark purple marking on the underside of its black abdomen. It wasn't fat, like an Earthling black widow. It had a fierce, agile look to it, like the raptor of spiders.

But, of course, this...*raptor spider* was the size of a dining room table. When it moved, I heard nothing but stillness, and yet the smallest glitter showed on one of its eight eyes. My hand was on my satchel, though I knew that everything useful had been removed from it.

Laurensen had the rifle raised, her finger poised over the trigger. She seemed to be counting, her breath steaming against the gun's side. Eerie's ears remained back, and when it swished its rudder-like tail, one of the scaled edges caught the back of my thigh.

"Go," Laurensen said.

I stared at her like she had lost her mind.

"Why?"

"I'll watch it."

"Shoot it," I breathed, voice barely audible.

"If I shoot it," she continued, breathing softly, "I will bring the attention of all kinds of hell down on us."

"So, you want to use me for bait?" I shook my head, correcting myself. "You want to see if it *eats* me?"

"She is territorial," Laurensen's eyes did not waver from the spider, but there was a sharpness in her voice that hadn't been there before. "She's defending her territory. I will put her down if she attacks you. Go."

"I don't believe that you're faster than that fucking spider," I muttered, fingers wriggling into fists.

The muscles of Laurensen's jaw flexed, and I felt a different kind of fear niggle at the back of my mind. I took a deep breath, stared at the spider for a moment more, and then began walking forward.

Between Laurensen's augmented rifle pointed toward my back and the fangs the length of my forearm above me, I thought it would be best if I stared at my feet. The earth was a purplish kind of black, soft and soaking. I listened with every fiber of my being. A thinner tree to my left twitched, and I nearly wet myself. The silence continued.

Adrenaline has a strange effect on time. For an hour, I felt like I'd been moving under the spider. And then, when I turned and found myself well around the bend in the river and unable to see Laurensen, it seemed to have passed in a handful of seconds.

The sniper appeared shortly after, walking backwards, Eerie at her side. The Nightmare tossed its head when it saw me, trotting the distance and shoving its scaled muzzle into my shoulder. I tottered, pressing my palm against its cheek reflexively, and the creature didn't seem opposed to the contact. My heart began beating again. I looked at Laurensen.

"That was fun," I growled.

She gave me a flat look as she slung the rifle across her back.

"I know," she answered.

There was a pause. And then, Laurensen's smile flashed. It was infinitely more wicked than any scowl she'd ever given me.

17

BESTIAL

It was raining again. Not hard, not even soaking. It was a wandering, bone-sucking kind of rain, where the mist collects just enough to run in rivulets through my hair. I watched it bead on the polished wood, tendrils breaking and following their own small rivulets along the rounded lid. It reminded me of blood.

The coffin was closed. Unity called it a security threat, but I knew the real reason. I had been the one who identified my brother's remains, after all.

Jerry tried to take my hand, but I was repelled by the gesture. It nauseated me for no reason. I was past needing reason. As I watched the coffin, something like pain squirmed behind my heart. It was longing, and nettled, and sharp. And I wanted to bleed.

But all there was, was rain.

* * *

"They used to call it the Meridiana Terra," Laurensen told me, nodding to the ocean. "Thought it was a plain."

"Things are never what you think they are," I answered around a mouthful of fruit.

We sat together and, despite my reservations from our last encounter with the like, we were on the edge of a cliff. Laurensen seemed a fan of heights, and I guess it was probably a result of her trade. She kept one knee up, boot propped against the cliff's rim, and the other leg dangled over the edge. Her rifle was across her lap. She grunted, eye still on the distant ocean.

"This isn't as sweet as I expected it would be," I said after a while, examining the core of the purple fruit I'd eaten. "It looked like a cross between a plum and a softball."

"Martian fruit," she said, shrugging.

I snorted, heaving the pit over the cliff's edge. It twisted down toward the canopy, some hundred meters beneath us.

"Don't mind me saying, but it's been three days," I told her, twisting to cross my legs. "Didn't you say that we were heading for a town?"

"Madtown," she said, though from her tone, I couldn't tell if she was acquiescing or correcting.

I gestured to the jungle surrounding us:

"It looks pretty wild around here."

"This ain't a Martian skyway, girl," she drew a deep breath, a finger tapping against her rifle's barrel. "It takes time."

"How much time?"

"On foot," Laurensen cocked her head, eyes narrowed. "Two weeks."

"*Two weeks*," I repeated, mouth hanging.

She arched a brow, looking at me for the first time.

"If you want to go running through the Martian jungle," she told me, spitting over the cliff, "I'm not going to stop you."

"That's not what I'm saying. But if we were supposed to rendezvous with Firebird, how long are they going to wait?"

"They won't wait. They'll arrive at Madtown in two days. If we're not there, they'll leave us."

I stared at her. I stared at her for long enough that if this would have been anyone else, they'd probably have slapped me by now. But not Laurensen. The woman had the gift of concentration, and she could ignore me as easily as I could ignore the air around us.

"So, we're fucked?"

"Might be."

Since staring at her wasn't doing any good, I twisted to stare at Eerie instead. It laid just behind us, wings tucked back, breath deep and calm. When I moved, it cracked an eyelid, the midnight-purple of its iris glittering like ink. My gaze moved to its shoulder, where the poultices Laurensen had applied still glistened against its injury.

"And there's no chance of us flying anywhere anytime soon," I mumbled, more to myself than to Laurensen.

"Not on Eerie," she said, laying back and putting her hat on her face, blocking both the sun and my inquisitive gaze.

"Not on Eerie," I repeated, irritated. "Then on what?"

She didn't answer. I scowled at the hat for a solid minute. Then, with resigned weariness, I stretched out my legs and eased back, looking at the sky instead. It was the light purple of midday, and I saw one of the moons—Phobos, I thought—skimming along the horizon.

"Do you ever wonder what they think," I said after a while. "The people we left behind?"

There was a noncommittal grunt under the hat, but I'd become accustomed to filling the silence by myself.

"I had a guy, for a while there," I said. "Jerry Harvard. It took me a long time to find someone who was good to me. I think, deep down, our instincts like the nasty ones. They'd be better at defending our young," I snorted. "One Evolutionary Psychology class in college, and I think I've figured out love. Jerry was different than the other guys. And a few girls, just after high school. You know how it is.

"The point is," I continued after a heavy sigh. "There was a day when I suddenly realized that I couldn't stand the sight of him. Isn't that strange? All that that boy ever did was love me, and I couldn't stomach the thought of his hand on mine. Maybe all we are is a desire to reproduce, after all, just a robot with sex drive and food for fuel."

Silence descended again. I twisted my satchel's strap.

"I don't miss him, but I do miss being with him. Sometimes. It's not a constant loneliness—I've always been better off alone. Sort of a continuing happiness and not something dependent on outside factors. But I miss the feeling of being in love. It's completing something that isn't broken, you know?"

The soft sound of a snore came out from under the hat.

"Yeah, I thought you would," I sighed.

When I rose, Eerie's eye opened to watch me. I nodded at it, picking up a long stick I'd found a while back and moving off to walk along the cliff's edge. If Laurensen planned to kill me in two days, it'd be to my own well-being to set out on my own. I'd learned a bit from her already, what fruits were safe and how to check for purple quicksand. And after the spider on the first day, our travels had been relatively unhindered by the local fauna (excepting one brief encounter with an Earth-like crocodile—apparently, those things had evolved to perfection already).

The cliff tapered off to a gravelly hill, the scrubby trees I'd been wandering through shifting to the taller, wiry versions of the canopy below. I squatted down, running my hand through the purplish soil. It had a strange, almost foam-like texture. The rocks and cliffs were shades of black, red, and purple. The very air had a sort of tint to it, like walking into a brightly painted room, and it made me lonely for Earth.

But, to be fair, I'd been lonely for Earth since the day we buried my brother.

Something snapped behind me. Instincts flared and I whirled, dropping to a crouch and whipping my walking staff around like a spear. I must have looked like some kind of cornered rat, all puffed up and making an attempt to look threatening. My teeth were even bared.

Eerie watched this with horse-like skepticism, the kind that they get when looking at the inside of a trailer for the first time. I sighed, dropping the staff and sitting back on my ass. Eerie took a step forward, muzzling my hair like a patch of questionable grass. I pushed its nose away before it could sample.

"At least I've made one friend," I said, pulling out a handful of the seeds I'd seen Laurensen feeding him.

Eerie's tongue was hot as it slobbered over my palm, picking up the round, black beads eagerly. The longer I knew it, the more horse-like it became. I cocked my head, looking between its legs. From my vantage point on the ground, I had a clear view of his equipment.

"And all this time," I said, scrubbing my slobbery hand against my thigh, "I thought that Redwing was a female-exclusive kind of ship."

Eerie, shoved at my shoulder, ears perked. I took a handful of his rubbery mane and used it to hoist myself onto my feet. As I turned to look toward the ocean again, leaning against my staff, Eerie began nosing around my side, smelling the seeds in my pocket.

And then, suddenly, he stopped. His head jerked back, neck arched, and he stared over the cliff. My guard instantly went up, and I froze beside him, grip tight on the staff.

"What," I started.

Eerie tossed his head, purplish eyes rolling, and when he screamed, it sent a river of ice down my back. His wings spread and a second later, he was on his hind legs, nearly bowling me over.

Worse still was the answering scream.

The Nightmares dove at us from behind, appearing over the trees. There were five of them, and the air shimmered with the refracted light of their dark scales. Eerie shrieked, fanning his wings, ears flat. The herd swept around us, circling like hawks before the dive.

I started running.

Eerie thundered behind me, the Nightmares screamed battle cries overhead, and my sole thought was that if I died here, my Martian headstone would read, *Trampled by horses.* Something hit my back and I went flying, staff bouncing from my hand as I hit the ground. I rolled, brought my arms over my face, and saw Eerie rearing over me, eyes wild. With his wings spread and his mane on end, he looked like a demon Pegasus.

Laurensen shouted. It wasn't a word, exactly. It was what an emotion would sound like. I rolled again, onto my belly, and I lifted my head to see her standing before me, one hand raised to the Nightmares in the sky. Her hat was gone, and her greasy brown hair jerked in the gale-force wind the Nightmares were kicking up. Her leather duster twisted around her ankles, and I was appalled to realize she didn't have her rifle.

"What are you—" with Laurensen, I was coming to realize that I rarely needed to complete my thoughts.

She shouted again, and again it was not a word. And then, the world quieted.

I was panting. I pushed myself to my knees, looking to the sky. The Nightmares continued to circle, but they were no longer screaming. Their wings were stretched with an almost lazy glide. Something tugged at my pocket and I looked to see Eerie, muzzling my thigh and looking for seeds.

"The fuck," I whispered, pushing myself to my feet and gathering up my staff.

The Nightmare herd circled lower. When they landed, it was as gently as a mother returning to her foal. They stood in a circle around us, sniffing at Eerie, who in turn took a curious bite at my pocket.

"The literal fuck," I turned to Laurensen.

Her hand was still raised, toward nothing in particular, and when I saw her eyes, ice plummeted into my gut.

They were distant, intent on something I could not see. They were darker without changing color. They were, in fact, the eyes of a BioMage.

Three of the Nightmares seemed to lose interest. They snorted, and when they galloped for the edge of the cliff and launched themselves into the sky, two remained. Laurensen's brow furrowed. She took a step forward, hand rotating so that her palm was up. The remaining Nightmares approached her slowly, not with caution but rather with curiosity. When they stopped, they stood on either side of her, heads slightly lowered, breathing soft and regular.

Laurensen lowered her hand, releasing a breath. She looked at me. Her eyes were still sharp, and I felt a distant, strange pressure against my forehead.

"You're a BioMage," I said.

"I'm not," she said, turning and walking toward where we had eaten our lunch.

The two Nightmares, Eerie, and I followed her. We watched her gather up her rifle and her hat. We watched her flip onto the new Nightmare's back. And while I watched her adjust her duster, the Nightmare pawed at the ground, as unconcerned as an old plow horse.

"Yes, you are," I argued, glowering at her. "You control animals. You're a Bestial BioMage."

"Piss off."

"If not, then how are you doing that?" I asked, ignoring Eerie's insistent nuzzling.

"Even in flight," she told me, tucking her hair back under the hat, "we'll need to push hard to make it to Madtown in time.

I glanced skeptically at the second Nightmare.

"You have to be a BioMage."

"Girl," she looked at me, and the pressure against my forehead increased—like a feather tickling my skull, "you got a death wish?"

18

MUTE

"No two BioMages are alike," it told me, slipping the IV's needle into my vein. *"Their influence varies, as do their specialties. It's like opening a Christmas present."*

I didn't think much of being opened at all. I stared at the white ceiling, felt an odd tingling of anticipation in my arm. I glanced at the needle, and watched a driblet of red run around the crease of my dark elbow.

"The so-called Firebird," the technician continued, soulless eyes swinging over my charts, *"is a BioMage of exceptional power, but her influence is restricted to a single will. She can force a new idea into people's minds, but she couldn't—say—read someone's thoughts. I,"* and it smiled its lifeless smile, *"have a certain aptitude for that. We have discovered BioMages in three categories: Empathic, Inceptive, and Bestial."*

"How long will you keep testing?" I asked, staring at a white light.

"However long it takes," it rapped a finger against my chart. *"I theorize that all Mutes have the potential to become BioMages. It's why Yo Ruse chose me to do the testing. As one of the Thirteen, your mother understands our—shall we say?— loopholes. It is my belief that we simply do not understand the kind of potential inherent in all BioMages—it's only a matter of time until we find yours."*

And then, the pain. It was blistering hot in my arm, like liquid fire ran into my veins. I began to scream, and my throat was already hoarse from it. I tried to run, but my arms and legs were fastened to the examination table. My flesh beneath the cuffs was bruised and bloody. My back arched as the fire spread, and my scream was something primal, something not quite of this world.

"Like opening a present," the technician said, hanging my chart on the bed's end.

* * *

Nightmares move in small herds. As Laurensen and I flew, I saw the three fellow creatures trail behind us. I couldn't tell if it was something Laurensen did, or if they followed because that was where their herd was going. In this world, I suppose that they were one and the same.

Martian jungle gave way to scrubby grassland. The soil changed from the deep purple to reddish dust, and it came much closer to fitting my idea of Mars. Laurensen kept our elevation at roughly a hundred meters, and the air was drier here. My face felt raw, and I tried to keep the collar of my shirt just below my eyes.

I could feel muscles in the Nightmare's back flexing, its wings wide and gossamer under the purple sky. My thighs were beyond aching. I'd ridden horses before, but never for this long, and certainly never with such paralyzing fear of falling. When a gust picked up, the Nightmare shifted, wings catching tendrils of stray air, and I clung to its rubber-like mane with raw, white fingers.

And the scales. I couldn't be sure, but I thought that the stickiness within my pants was more than sweat. As we flew, I considered the possibility of my never walking again.

We made ten stops, all told. Laurensen watered the horses in streams. When she drank, she dipped her entire face in the water, hat held to her head. I didn't understand why she didn't take it off until we were in the air again. I certainly wished I had something damp and cool against my brow.

My first glimpse of Madtown was something of a hallucination. It took perhaps an hour before I realized that the boulders we were flying toward were actually red huts. As we descended, I had the uncomfortable feeling that we were entering a ghost town. There were perhaps fifty of the huts, short and markedly without windows or doors, and there was not a human in sight.

Laurensen landed a second before me, the Nightmare galloping as its hooves touched down, and her duster billowed dramatically in her wake. When I landed, the jolt sent me forward, and I managed to crack my nose against the back of the creature's skull.

And so, broken and literally bleeding, I entered Madtown.

Laurensen led the way through the buildings, rifle slung across her back, hat low and handkerchief pulled up to her eyes. My Nightmare trotted to her side, stepping in with its companion in perfect tandem. I looked at Laurensen.

"Where is everyone?" I croaked.

She didn't look at me. And she didn't answer. These were things I had grown accustomed to. What I wasn't accustomed to, however, was the quiet tension that surrounded her. Rawn Laurensen had a way of looking at every problem with disdain, and it was oddly calming.

Here, I saw her eyes flick over the vacant buildings with the quick sharpness of a predator suddenly turned prey. She had a hand on the pistol at her hip, and the other remained frozen against her thigh. I could see that her pants were faded and worn there. I tried to swallow, but there was only dust in my mouth.

A shadow passed over me, and I looked up to see Eerie still in the air. He had flown at Laurensen's side for the duration of our journey. I glanced again at the sniper.

"What's wrong?"

Instead of answering, she drew our Nightmares to a sudden halt. At first, I thought it was out of frustration toward me, but when I followed her gaze, I saw that we had come to the end of Madtown. I frowned at the ground perhaps fifty meters in front of us. It took me a minute to see what Laurensen had focused on.

There was a trench. It stretched from right to left, bordering Madtown. The slope across the gap was gradual enough that I could barely distinguish it.

The Nightmares suddenly spread their wings. I had a moment of lurching devastation—I'd give almost anything to lay on the ground and not move for three days—but it quickly curdled to fear as Laurensen pulled the revolver. She didn't give me time for another question. Instead, the Nightmares launched themselves forward.

It wasn't a long flight. We half galloped, half glided to the edge of the trench. And when the beasts vaulted over the edge, the ground dropped away. The best way that I could describe it is if we were sitting on a massive shelf and suddenly dropped over the edge. The ground plunged perhaps fifty meters straight down. The opposite edge of the trench was a gradual slope. Lauresen twisted our flight and we descended smoothly.

Facing the shelf, I realized two things. Firstly, the slope was a landing strip into a cavern. Secondly, and more importantly, Madtown was not deserted. Laurensen and I glided into the mouth of the cavern, but it was not dark. The lights were orange, and thousands of them dangled from the ceiling of the cavern. It cast the city within in a perpetual, reddish light.

What I had mistaken for huts were in fact the tops of buildings. I could not determine the size of the cavern—it was literally an underground city. We flew just above the landing strip, gliding toward what looked like a huge used car lot. Only, instead of cars, there were spaceships. Beyond the spaceships, the mouth of the city was barred like a prison's cell.

Laurensen flew over the ships and landed just outside the city gate. When she dismounted, it was before the Nightmare had entirely stopped running, and she twisted to the ground with the cool security of a long-time rodeo performer. Her Nightmare didn't pause. In fact, the second her boots touched the earth, it tossed its head and shrieked.

Mine followed suit, and I threw myself off the creature a moment before it vaulted back into the air, screaming at the world. The two bolted toward the mouth of the cavern, wings pumping furiously.

I hadn't landed with an inkling of the grace Laurensen displayed. I stared at her from the ground, my pants ripped, my legs and hands bleeding, and I wondered if I had saliva enough to swear. Laurensen still held the revolver, and she spared me the smallest of glances before she turned to Madtown's gate.

The bars of the blockade were as thick as my waist, set too far apart to keep a human from squeezing through, but plenty close to keep the ships surrounding us from entering. I pulled my knees under myself, wincing as my beaten muscles stretched in new ways.

"Hell take me," a man's voice growled. "I can't believe my fucking eyes."

I turned. Laurensen faced the gates, revolver pointed at a man's head. He had the look of a security officer, though he wore no discernable uniform, and the fire-based shotgun he held bespoke business. He scowled at Laurensen.

"Afternoon," she said, cocking the revolver.

"I'm going to blow you into orbit," he spat, pumping the shotgun and levelling it at Laurensen's chest.

"You think you're fast enough for that?" I couldn't see her face, but I knew well the way she would be arching a brow.

"Bitch, Overlord Shay *told* you what would happen if you came back here."

"My contract was fulfilled," she said, taking a step to the side, angling her head.

"Sure. And the second it was, you turned around and joined the fucking enemy."

"My contract was fulfilled," she repeated. "My next one had to begin."

"Goddamned assassins," he looked at me for the first time. "You don't have the backup for your mouth, Rawn."

Two figures appeared behind the guard, flanking him with shotguns raised. I heard something behind me and I turned to find myself staring down the barrel of a fourth gun. The man holding it smiled at me, a single tooth revealing itself.

"Laurensen," I breathed.

"If Shay has a problem with me," Laurensen said, not looking away from the initial guard, "that's her problem. Her contract was fulfilled, and so my integrity remains intact. I'm a gun for hire. If she wanted loyalty," and it was her turn to spit, "she should have hired her mother."

"Damned assassins," the guard growled again. He nodded.

The guard closest to me seized my arm and hauled me to my feet. It was just as well, since I doubted I could have managed it on my own, but his fingers were short and callused, and they dug into the meat of my bicep. I swore, jerking my arm, but he merely gave it a twist.

"What's the plan then?" Laurensen asked, cool as an autumn morning.

"I'm going to take your friend," he snorted, "to the Overlord. And I'm going to have her carry your head in a basket."

"That's what I thought," she said.

Something in the air changed. It was static. It made my hair stand on end, my flesh coming alive with sensation. My body hurt in a way that it had never hurt before.

Every BioMage is different.

Laurensen's revolver went off and I jumped just as hard as the guard holding me. Laurensen's powder-based weapon blew a neat hole through the initial guard's forehead, blood and brains exploding out the back of his skull—*hollow point, classic powder-base.*

Three more shots cracked. Laurensen turned smoothly, fired quickly, and had twisted toward me in the space of five heartbeats, the three guards at the gates dropping as she did so. Her duster billowed—somewhat dramatically, I have to admit—and when she aimed at the guard holding me, he began to tremble.

"*Stop*," he snarled, shotgun held awkwardly at my side.

His hand was around my throat, and it kept my head in front of his. I stared down the barrel of Laurensen's gun. It was a position I was becoming altogether too familiar with, and irritation bubbled deep within me.

"If you were going to shoot her," I said, voice like sandpaper, "you'd have already done it."

The static in the air intensified. The guard holding me was sweating. He smelled like an old, dirty towel. The hand on my throat tightened, and small dots swirled in my peripherals. So, I heard rather than saw two more guards come up next to us.

"This is bullshit," I said, scowling at Laurensen.

Logic, my brother told me once, is a double-edged sword. On the one hand, I was often right. On the other, people rarely enjoy being proven wrong.

My irritation, edged in fear, was the perfect ammunition. Even as the guard squeezed the life from me, I built an image in my mind. The static in the air intensified. Through the darkness, Laurensen's figure sharpened. I took my fury, my fear, my sheer bloody *indignation*, twisted them in my mind and I—

—*pushed.*

Every BioMage is different, sure. But in all of the worlds, never has there been a BioMage like *me*. I could feel the metal on the man. It was like acid against my flesh. I could smell it in the air, sense it surrounding me.

His shotgun, the bullets at his belt, the keys in his pocket—every metallic thing he had suddenly was repelled from each other, as though they had abruptly turned into the worlds' most powerful magnets. He gasped as his rings ripped his fingers away. Literally, ripped them away. Blood sprayed from his broken stumps.

I was shoved away from him, the metal on my own person reacting similarly. I slammed against Laurensen. She didn't seem surprised, and her sudden fall meant that the two shots from the flanking guards went over our heads. Laurensen caught her balance, came up spinning, and shot the guard on her right.

I rolled to the side, snatched up a fallen shotgun, and put the first round through the guard to my left. His chest exploded in red, the fire-based gun igniting him from within. Laurensen continued her turn, stopping with the revolver aimed at me.

We stared at each other for a second, guns poised. The static surrounding me was an aura, and I saw it lift stray thread and dust from Laurensen's mantle. I pushed against her, ever so lightly, shifting her aim. She frowned at me.

"What would be the point?" I asked her, lowering my shotgun, flexing my power.

Laurensen's chapped lips turned toward a smile. With a snort, she pointed the gun at the ground, spun the chamber, and set to reloading. When she finished, she met my eye. She slipped the revolver slowly back into its holster.

"Don't much need a point, anymore."

19

MADTOWN

The first time I used my power, I killed someone. As I've said, I couldn't determine the sex of my technician, so in my mind, I murdered it. That eased my guilt. Killing it is very different than killing her.

Still, the way I ripped its head apart with the metal implants is something that I can't forget. I can't forget anything, after all. And so, I remember the way my mother looked at me when she entered the room and saw the remains of the technician on the floor.

Sometimes, I vomit when I remember the way she smiled.

* * *

"Madtown," Laurensen said, walking at my side, "is the oldest Martian settlement."

"Population 37,000," I said, resting a hand on the top of my satchel. "Founded by the 300 Initiates."

She nodded, gesturing to the tall, wandering buildings that seemed to grow from the edges of the street we walked on. They had been carved from the red rock, and they were wandering columns between the floor and the ceiling.

"My question," I continued, "is what happened to Overlord Rowan."

"Dead," she said.

"I ascertained as much. *How* is the question."

She looked at me, and those cracked lips twisted again. Beneath the hat's brim, her green and blue eyes glinted ominously in the orangish light.

"Someone went and shot him," she said.

I nodded.

Madtown was simultaneously slower and louder than Biggie's Chryse. Instead of a massive skyway, transportation was limited to foot travel and small, low-grade hovercrafts. There didn't seem to be any rhyme or reason to the streets, merely constant vigilance and good reflexes. Laurensen and I walked in a river of humanity, and the world around us was orange light and *sound*.

Instead of the universal music that Biggie's Chryse provided, Madtown was a cacophony of song. There were live bands on almost every corner, and their quality varied widely. A few screeched out old-time fiddle tunes more suited to the of-then United States cultures, and a few more took a stab at the retro-swing favored in the Chryse.

I saw horses tethered outside more than a few bars, and they were Earthier than the Nightmares Laurensen and I had ridden. Their coats were rubbery, and their manes had the same, spikey look as Nightmares, but their tails remained hair and their backs were decidedly free of wings.

"Fresh blood, unnaturally selected," Laurensen told me, when she saw me staring. "Some people prefer the classics."

"Strange of them," I muttered, sidestepping a man who seemed uninterested in allowing me my space.

Laurensen nodded.

"Where are we going?" I asked her.

"Little pub in the Deeps," she said. "If they're here, that's where they'll be."

"What's it called?"

She cocked a brow at me. We didn't slow, but for several strides, we stared at each other. When a hovercraft made to run us over, Laurensen took me by the shoulder and guided me to the edge of the street. Something about the way she held herself made other people move out of her way. Walking on sidewalks had long been a strange social dynamic, and it has long divided humanity into two groups: those who defer, and those who do not.

"I'm forty-six years old," Laurensen told me, hand still on my shoulder. "I've been a gun for hire for thirty of those years. How long do you think I would have lasted, if I trusted people?"

"That's fair," I said, not looking at her as I pulled away from her grip. "And you've got less call to trust me than most people. But if you tell me where I can find them, I'm not going to fucking kill you."

"It's what I would do," she chuckled, dark and low. "You've got a fifty-fifty chance of them being there. If they aren't, I'm going to kill you and sever my contract. But if you kill me first, you've got the odds on your side."

"Maybe," I shrugged. "But the thing is, without you watching my back, I'm probably not going to make it through Madtown. So, the odds are about the same."

Laurensen paused at that.

"I fucking hate math," she said.

"We've finally found something we can agree on, then."

And so, the assassin and I walked the Martian streets. I kept my head low, avoiding eye contact, and Laurensen kept her hat near her eyes, bulling through the crowd. We walked in the same way, and yet our walks were entirely different.

"You hide it well," the sniper told me as we turned down a narrow alley.

"What?"

"Your BioMage."

I twisted my satchel's strap. When I shrugged, she didn't look at me.

"I shouldn't be one."

She nodded.

"And yet, here we are. Why do you hide it?"

"You know how Unity is. As far as I know, I'm the first adaption of telekinesis in history. BioMages shouldn't be able to alter the physical world. The fact that I can...well, what's different about my DNA? And, more to the point, what would they do to me to find out?"

It was a lie, and Laurensen could hear it. But instead of calling it, she kept her silence. We stepped through an archway and began to descend a wide, wandering ramp. Hovercrafts gave way to robotics, physically attached to the wall like a ski lift. Most of the people walked.

"Why hide it from us?" she asked after a long while.

"Same reason."

She shook her head.

"You could have used it to escape."

"You say that like I don't want to be here. Actually riding with..." I stopped myself from saying *Firebird*, my eyes flicking over the humanity surrounding us. "Actually riding with them is the best way for me to continue reporting on her achievements. How do you know that I wasn't planning on freeing her and joining the crew all along?"

"Because," and she slipped a wicked look at me, "she had to pull too many strings to make sure you'd be the one to meet her."

I frowned at that.

"But if all that she wanted was to—"

Someone crashed into me. I fell hard, my legs stiff and my body wrung dry, and when the woman grabbed my satchel and took off up the street, all that I managed was a cry of outrage. Laurensen watched it happen, her hand on her revolver, and she drew two settling breaths before she drew the weapon.

"Jesus Christ," I said, standing in time to grab her wrist.

She cocked that frosty brow, and I found the gesture irrationally irritating.

"You don't have to fucking shoot all of your problems," I told her, releasing her wrist. "There was nothing in it that I can't live without. And certainly nothing in it worth her dying for."

She shrugged, holstering her weapon with a *your loss* kind of expression. I glanced once after the thief, but she was long gone. When we resumed our walk, I glowered at anyone bold enough to meet my eye.

"You've had training," she told me.

"It's that obvious?" I muttered, moving to rest my hand on my satchel and grinding my teeth when I found nothing there.

"With your power," she said, hooking a thumb in her gun belt, "you could have gotten your bag back yourself."

"I could have. But why does that make you think I've had training?"

"Fresh BioMages don't have the control to focus their will. They merely want, and their bodies move to achieve it. Same as instinctively trying to catch a dropped knife. You don't register that you'd be better off letting it fall, not until you cut yourself a few times."

"You're smarter than you look," I told her.

She gave me a surprised look.

"It's the hat, isn't it?"

I stared at her for a while. And when she laughed, it made me flinch.

"You know, you're growing on me, kid," she slapped a palm against my back. "And I'm just a hired gun. So, keep in mind that if you cross her while my contract is live, I'm going to put you down *hard*."

I shoved my hands violently into my pockets.

"I'm not crossing anyone, Rawn. Just trying to live my life."

"Sure," she said, her hand twisting and seizing the back of my shirt, stopping me.

I moved to push her away, but instead found myself looking down the barrel of her revolver. I lost sensation in my limbs, adrenaline flooding through me. It was electric, and when the static filled the air between us, it was strong enough that the handkerchief around her neck lifted.

She arched that damned brow again, and my eyes had a chance to really focus on her gun. She wasn't pointing it at me. Rather, just past my left ear.

"Feeling lucky?" she asked someone behind me.

"Getting lucky all the time," a familiar voice answered.

Laurensen's smile sent a simultaneous burst of relief and fury through me, and I shoved her away from me. I turned to find Ori leaning in an open doorway, assault rifle pointed lazily at the sniper. In her other hand, she held a half-eaten apple. She grinned at me.

"Never thought I'd see you again, pup," she told me, taking another bite. The rifle's butt rested casually against her hip, and neither she nor Laurensen made a move to lower their guns. "Damned near a miracle."

"You always welcome your friends like this?" I asked her, feeling plenty frustrated.

"We ain't none of us friends," Ori informed me.

She had her bowler hat on, and she'd exchanged the suit for a dark shirt, pants and suspenders. The gun belt around her waist had long, vicious-looking bullets in it, as well as a sawed-off shotgun on each hip. When she smiled, there were apple bits in her teeth.

"For fuck's sake," I growled, once again trying to rest my hand on my satchel.

"You find Jacobs?" Laurensen asked, her eyes a dark glitter beneath the hat's brim.

Ori's grin widened, white in her black face.

"Nope."

Laurensen nodded. And then she and Ori both lowered their weapons.

"Never can be too safe," Ori informed me with a wink. "In you go."

I glowered at her.

"Even if her contract was up," I said, jerking my chin toward Laurensen. "You've got no call to shoot me."

"Never know," she winked at me, tossing the apple's core across the street.

I swore at Ori as I shouldered past her. I'd had just about my fill of working with assassins and thieves.

Madtown was carved from Martian stone, and the rocks were red like sandstone. The orange lights outside gave everything a bloody cast, and the blue lights within shed a purplish hue. The pub smelled strongly of tobacco and booze, and the underlying stench of slow-moving air made my nose dry.

I'd barely gotten through the doorway before there was a *squee* of surprise. Brute collided with me a second later, Jiggy's gravitational arms squeezing the air from my lungs.

"I *knew* you'd make it," she told me, her lights whirling bright and yellow. "I told them, and no one would believe me! I should have put some credits on it. You're tougher than you look, I told them. I'm so happy to be right!"

I patted Jiggy's round, cool side and tried a smile on for size. It hurt my chapped lips.

"It's good to see you too, Brute."

"Those murders, they're really something, aren't they?" she asked me, gravity arms pulling me away from the door and toward the bar. "Just the worst. I've had a few run-ins with them before by myself. Chased me all the way into Biggie's Chryse, once. Just the absolute worst."

Regina was alone at the bar, a delicate glass in her big hand, and when she saw me, she grunted.

"Isn't it a miracle," Brute asked her, bobbing against Regina's shoulder.

"Fucking Christmas come early," Regina told her, taking a small sip from the long-stemmed, fluted glass.

"Is that champagne?" I asked, staring at her.

"It's the only thing she likes!" Brute informed me.

"So what if it is?" Regina growled, ignoring Brute, her scowl reserved solely for me.

I decided to leave that alone, though the image of Regina sipping anything daintily was a contradiction that hurt my brain. I asked the barkeep—an aging man with strange, purplish eyes—for the biggest glass of water he had. And then, pitcher in hand, I left Regina to her champagne. I passed Margaret, her red hat low and her glass of whiskey in hand, and found Harry and Firebird near the back of the room.

The women turned to me as I sat at their table. Harry's smile did not touch her eyes. I chugged water, letting it spill down my front. I chugged until the pitcher was half empty and I could feel the liquid sloshing in my gut. And then, I sat it on the table, leaned forward, stared Firebird right in the face, and said:

"I'm a spy."

20

INCEPTIVE

The proposition hung in the room. My mother's mouth was twisted, as though the taste of it had left something bitter on her tongue. There were guards in all four corners of the small, windowless enclosure. There was a low, metal table in the center. I sat on one side, and Yo Ruse sat on the other.

I stared at my mother, one of the Thirteen Yo. She did not wear the metal marks of her office. In fact, she wore no metal at all. She knew what I was.

"You thought of this on your own?" she asked.

My mother had two tones. There was the one she used exclusively on me and, when he was alive, my brother. And then, there was this one. The voice of the Yo. The voice of one of the thirteen most powerful people in Unity.

"I'm an independent woman," I told her. "I don't take advice from anyone, and I work for my own will."

"Will is subject to change," Yo Ruse told me. "Even for Mutes. There are classic techniques. What you propose, Yin Lurk, requires a level of skill that I doubt you've had the time to obtain. How old are you?"

She obviously knew how old I was.

"Twenty-six," I sneered, and her mouth remained twisted.

"Twenty-six," Yo Ruse leaned back, her long, slender, white-clad body the opposite of relaxed.

"I'm an old soul," I told her, my humor dry and ill-fitted to the room. My mother's look of scorn made me smile. "And I'm your only option."

* * *

The way Firebird looked at me now reminded me of *Yo* Ruse in ways that made me uncomfortable. People of great power have an aura about them. They don't only expect to be obeyed, they rarely consider the potential for failure. It's not who they are, even if they are not someone they were meant to be.

"A spy," Firebird said.

I felt no pressure against my brow. A BioMage of her power shouldn't be able to leave a Mute—as all BioMages are Mute to one another—completely untouched. And yet, Firebird's will was iron-clad. I nodded.

Harry's eyes held a deep kind of sorrow. She reminded me of a woman who has given up on love, who has been hurt so often that there is nothing else to expect from people. She hadn't given up—instead, she simply accepted that there is no such thing as success. All things sour in time, love and hearts lost under the millstone.

At least, that's what people believe while they are in the fresh throws of pain. Afterwards, with the benefit of time and space, we begin to feel better for it. It follows us through our lives, lessons learned and pain accepted.

"Then you're not a very good one," Harry said.

The pilot wore a suit's vest, and she reached within to reveal a small pistol—*acid-based.* I didn't look at it when she rested the butt on the table, barrel pointed at my chest.

Firebird's hands were on the table, and when she tapped her fingers, it was with a smooth, wave-like motion of all ten digits. She repeated this three times. And when she stopped, the room seemed to quiet a little around us. I didn't need to turn to know that Regina was behind me.

"Why?" Firebird asked.

"Because you already knew," I told her.

She paused. Harry glanced at her, surprise flashing behind her eyes when Firebird nodded.

"You knew?" Harry asked her, and her voice was thin.

"I did."

"And you brought her on *Redwing* anyway?" Harry's words snapped against her teeth, and fury tightened her expression. I gaped at her, surprised at the sudden vehemence. For a second, I thought that she might shoot us both.

Firebird raised a finger, not looking at Harry. She held my gaze like a cat watches a mouse. I smiled at her.

"You thought that you could change my mind," I told her. "As a BioMage, you can't help yourself. It's how the world works. You thought that if I got to know your crew, I'd get a solid dose of Stockholm Syndrome and turn on Unity."

Firebird didn't answer. And the muscles in Harry's jaw tightened. The end of her pistol quivered when she said:

"You let another *fucking* spy on my ship."

"A fucking *what*?" Regina asked from behind me.

Her voice made my hackles raise, but I did not look away from Firebird. I laid my hands flat on the table.

"I was going to wait. But when someone—I'm going to guess Brute—had my satchel stolen, my time was broken. You knew, but you didn't tell your crew. Brute would have realized that I used her computers. I didn't have time to wipe my fingerprints from the system. If the crew suspected me, they'd kill me.

"You want me because I'm a BioMage, so I'd be no good to you dead. Except for the tests that you would have Doctor Ravin run on me. So, I—"

"She's a goddamned BioMage," Regina snarled.

Her big hand came down around the back of my neck, and she began to lift me from the table. I gave Firebird a second. Just the one, before I would split the she-hulk in half with the metal clasp on her belt. It was all that Firebird needed.

When she raised a hand from the table, Regina froze, still holding me slightly off my chair. Static surrounded me, mounting on the tension, building in my veins. Harry's eyes flicked to Firebird. The room was silent.

"You," Firebird said, standing, "are a BioMage?"

I paused. My stomach did a horrible, lurching thing, like it would if I missed a step on my way downstairs. I stared at her.

"I knew you were a spy," she told me, fingers resting on Harry's pistol, pushing it away from me.

"But then why?" my throat was raw. "Why'd you take me on, if you didn't need me as a BioMage? Surely all of that about needing a journalist...surely that isn't the reason you—"

A gunshot cracked behind me. Regina's hand vanished, and I threw myself to the side, rolling across the rough stone floor. Harry leapt to her feet, a snarl erupting from her lips. I looked to the door and saw a plainly dressed man there, his pistol levelled at Firebird. He wore a visor. Regina hit the floor a second later, her body writhing as she gasped, a hand against her chest.

The shot had gone clean through her. The room paused, thirty people realizing what had happened at the same time. I looked at Firebird. And, for a second, Firebird looked at me. Then, the other patrons in the bar stood. Visors appeared in their hands, and they snapped them over their foreheads and eyes. They pulled guns from within their coats.

And they pointed them at Firebird.

"*Fucking spy*," Harry screamed, her pistol jerking down toward me.

I'd never been one for timing.

"Stop," Firebird said.

And, though I felt no inkling of power from Firebird, Harry stopped. She glanced at her leader, the gun still pointed at my head. Firebird looked at me. Static filled the room. I could *taste* the metal. There was so much of it. My will crackled just beneath my flesh.

Firebird's eyes moved from me to the plain-clothed man. She was unconcerned by the number of guns pointed at her. Margaret, still in the corner, had a hand under the table. I looked at the doorway, but neither Ori nor Laurensen lurked there. Either they had been killed, or they'd let the men through. Either way, they wouldn't be much help.

"I don't think that I know you," Firebird said.

"Martian Agent Rathe," he told her, one hand darting into his pocket for a Unity badge.

"Ah. I've been expecting you," she said, calm and cool. "It took you longer than I would have thought."

"I'd put you down right here and now," he told her. "But I expect that whatever tests command is planning for you will be far worse than a bullet."

"I'm impressed by the number of men you managed to secret past the Martian government," Firebird continued. "Unity is less welcome here than even I am."

"Put your fucking hands in the air," he told her, taking a step closer.

My heart thundered against my ribs. My will trembled within me, near bursting, and if I unleashed now, with so many fingers on triggers, God only knew who'd be killed. I raised a hand slowly from the floor. Power crackled. I wasn't breathing. I tried to, and I nearly choked.

"I do hate visors," Firebird said, closing her eyes. "You are without souls, when you hide behind their eyes."

The air in the room...*changed.* I could not describe it. It was a shift as subtle and ancient as falling in love. My hearing seemed to get better and worse at the same time, my heart like thunder while the room seemed filled with water.

And the armed men, their visor-blinded gazes still on Firebird, moved as a unit. Some fought, a few screamed, but their pistols shifted from Firebird, to the underside of their own chins. Agent Rathe's arm quivered as he did the same, and his teeth bared.

"Impossible," he snarled.

Firebird stared at him. She raised a hand slowly, making a finger gun at the Agent. She cocked her thumb, and mouthed:

"Bang."

And, in the end, Rathe was the only man who did not pull the trigger.

21

DRAGONS

"You will lose everything," Agent Rathe had told me. "The ultimate sacrifice. If you aren't willing to commit your life— your soul—then you have no business here."

The room was small and stark, not unlike the man in front of me. I crossed my legs. It felt wrong. I straightened. I put both feet on the floor. I stared through him, to a time when this wouldn't have happened.

To a time when nothing ever did, really.

"It's all I have left," I whispered.

My brain hurt. Not my head, nothing so simple as a headache. My brain ached. It was deep and throbbing, like I had just crammed for an exam. My will was worn feather-thin and I couldn't have attempted MetalMage if my life depended on it.

MetalMage. That was what they were calling it now. Before, there hadn't been a name. There hadn't needed to be. Because, before my training, there hadn't been a MetalMage.

"You will die," he told me. "The rebel X is ruthless."

"I know," I snapped. My eyes flashed to his, and something deep and twisted heated my core.

"Unity is not depending on you," he informed me. "Unity exists as a whole, an entity without flaw. Your assistance in this is wholly your doing. Unity would not owe

you, would not pay you. Your assistance would never be known."

"Yours would," I said.

"Mine will. I am an Enforcer. We are the law, and when a rebel arises, we destroy them. Do you understand?"

I'd understood all along. And when I nodded, the throbbing in my skull was thunder to my pain.

* * *

"*HANDS IN THE AIR,*" Harry screamed.

I felt the barrel of her pistol against the small of my back, and when I put my hands in the air, she shoved me against the wall. There was blood on it. There was blood on everything. And I'd be lying if I said I didn't gag.

Harry ripped a pair of cuffs from the bodies of one of the Unity soldiers, and when she clamped the smooth metal around my wrists, it was tight enough that I'd lose all sensation within the hour. She grabbed my shoulder and threw me toward the door. I stumbled over a body, and without my arms, I fell face-first beside Agent Rathe.

He was immobile, his hand clenching the revolver still under his own chin, and when our eyes met, I could see *pain*. Oh God, the *pain*. They were the eyes of a man who had just killed his only son, an accident that reveals itself a second too late. His panic laid there, bared of the visor. I saw it, useless and broken, laying on the floor among his fallen soldiers.

"Get to the ship," Firebird told Harry, calm as dawn. "Get her ready."

"Ori," Harry started, gun still pointed at me as she looked to Firebird.

"I will take care of Ori." Firebird's gaze fell on me. "Go."

Harry didn't hesitate again. She shoved the pistol into her belt and took off through the open doorway. She'd forgotten her hat.

"Margaret," Firebird said.

The areologist still sat at her table in the corner. Her hat was pulled low over her eyes, and when Firebird said her name, a shudder went through her body. The voice of a BioMage always carries will, a desire for something, and even if she didn't intend to subject her power, it was there.

Margaret leaned back in her chair, one hand on the tumbler of whiskey, and she regarded the room with dark eyes. When her gaze found me, cuffed and covered in other people's blood, she sighed.

"You know my demands," she said, looking away.

"And they are met," Firebird agreed. "Take a shuttle to the shipyard. Walk to *Redwing* independently."

"Naturally," she agreed, sipping the whiskey. "Did you know?"

"I know everything," Firebird took a gun from the corpse of a soldier, checked the magazine—*standard issue, electric-based, nonlethal*—and nodded to Margaret. "Please."

The areologist considered the rebel for a moment that was much too long. And then, she tossed the whiskey back, stood carefully, and stepped through the room. She kept her jacket over an arm, and she didn't touch a body. When she was gone, the atmosphere in the room shifted again.

Beside me, Agent Rathe began to growl. Blood trickled from one of his nostrils. I could see the panic, flaring brighter behind his eyes, and when he stood, it was with tears on his cheeks. The Agent pulled a key card from the back of his belt and tapped it against my manacles. They sprang open and he began to growl, low in the back of his throat. He left me then, standing in a corner by the door, unnaturally still.

I looked at Firebird, my mouth hanging open.

"You're letting me go?" I asked her.

The rebel leader regarded me. Her reptilian eyes were flat, almost as lifeless as Rathe's were terrified. She drew a slow breath.

"I do not subject my will on any under my command," she told me. "They are here on their own accord. You may find that difficult to believe, but I do not lie. I do not need to, not when I am who I am."

"Okay," I said, pushing myself cautiously to my feet. She made no move to stop me. In fact, despite the residual essence of BioMage will left in the room, I could not sense her will.

"I know what you are, Jezi Lurk. Perhaps even better than you do. And I know what I need from you cannot be obtained without your Unity resources. I do not need you for your mother," she continued when I opened my mouth, fear kindling deep within me. "I need you for *you*, the same as the rest of my crew."

"But I am not part of your crew. For Christ's sake, Firebird," I spread my hands. "I'm your *enemy*."

A small, twisted smile haunted her lips.

"You are many things. That is not among them. Come," she nodded. "If we are not in the ship within the hour, our lives are forfeit."

"Why?"

She stared at me.

"You will want a weapon," she said as means of answer.

I felt the smallest pressure against my third eye, and Agent Rathe moved through the door, motions jerky and inconsistent, more like a robot than a man. I hesitated before throwing myself at one of the dead soldiers. I found a pistol like the one Firebird had looted, and I checked its chamber before following Rathe out of the door.

The first thing that I saw was Ori. She laid on her side, blood running from a gash in the side of her head. The second was that the once-bustling street was now deserted. I turned, gun held to the side, my finger on the trigger, and watched Firebird emerge from the pub. She went to a knee in a smooth motion, checked Ori's pulse with quick, sure fingers. When she nodded, Rathe seized her limp form and hauled her into a fireman's carry. His knees trembled, and blood continued to run from his nose. It leaked into his mouth, but he did not wipe it away.

"This way," Firebird said, leading up the street at a brisk walk.

"He wasn't supposed to be here," I told her, my eyes darting over the buildings.

"Unity never was supposed to exist. We cannot predict something so unnatural," she told me.

"You didn't seem surprised, though."

"I expect the worst in every scenario," she told me. "This was a possibility, and a lesser one at that."

She paused. Then:

"*Down!*"

I was already on edge, so I dropped nearly instantaneously. It was still barely fast enough. I felt more than heard the gun go off, and a flash of fire left a streak of white across my vision. Firebird was already poised, dropped to one knee and aiming just over my head. She froze for half a heartbeat. And when she shot, it was with such certainty that she was already standing before the *crack* of the electric-based pistol had entirely left my hearing.

I stood shakily, and when she grabbed my arm, it was to get me running. Side by side, Firebird and I tore up the street. Agent Rathe followed at my flank, puffing and wheezing. I could see his face turning a horrible shade of red.

"Who is shooting at—" I started.

Firebird's grip tightened, and she wrenched me to the side as another gun went off. I saw the muzzle flash this time, and the figure behind it was tall and dressed in black.

"Unity," I panted. "They're Unity *Dragons*."

"They are," she said, voice cool. She wasn't even winded.

"Oh, fuck me," I said, stumbling after her up a series of narrow, filthy stairs. "Oh, fuck me sideways. They don't miss!"

"They just did," she informed me.

She had a point. As we exited the alley, I found myself hunched and ready to drop. Firebird straightened when she started to sprint. I felt like a fish out of water as I floundered after her, puffing every bit as hard as Agent Rathe. He began to pass me. Ori's head bobbed madly against his back. Blood splattered the street after him. My lungs were on fire. And still, Firebird ran.

Force slammed against my third eye. It was as sudden and unexpected as a truck in the wrong lane, and it hit me head-on. I screamed when I fell, my hands flying over my forehead. The ground hit me too many times as I thudded to a stop against the stairs. The pain amplified and I shrieked, back arching, eyes blinded by white, *blistering* light. It sharpened, a dagger against my skull. I had never, not in all the tests that Unity had run, not in all my life felt such *pain.*

The problem with being a Mute or a BioMage is that while other BioMages cannot force themselves into your mind, their will is more than an idea. It can still *hurt.* It can still push, and when it meets with resistance, they react as any creature would.

They push *harder.*

I heard another scream. The pressure lessened. And then, there were a chorus of screams. They rose to a pitch that reverberated in the Martian air. And the pressure dissolved.

I was panting. When I rolled to my hands and knees, my elbows nearly buckled. I l looked up and saw Firebird standing in front of me, her eyes wide and nearly black, her hands at her sides. Agent Rathe stood beside her, and his gaze was vacant. The blood under his nose had dried.

Around us, I saw black-wrapped Unity Dragons.

They were assassins. They were officials. They were whatever Unity needed them to be, and their training allowed for all situations. They were snipers, fighters, and BioMages.

And they were dead.

I stood, counting. Twelve Dragons surrounded us, some of them half falling from the balconies they'd been hiding on. Others laid in the street, broken and bleeding. Firebird looked at me.

"Thirteen. There will be thirteen," I wheezed, my brain something like twisted agony.

"Thirteen," she agreed, her hands lowering.

She blinked, and I saw some of the will behind her eyes fade. The pressure against my forehead was tickling and sickly. She blinked again. When she looked at Agent Rathe, something like agony slipped across her face, slippery and elusive as the shadow of a shark.

When we began running, Agent Rathe's movements were fluid. It was not the jerky run of a man fighting. It was as fast as it was lifeless. Firebird increased the pace and suddenly, it was all that I could think about. It was the kind of sprint that requires body, mind, and soul. It was the kind of sprint that can only last for a few blocks, the kind that pulls everything from your muscles and then some.

It was a sprint like I had never known, and my vision blackened around the edges.

When we burst free of Madtown's gate, something in my legs gave out and I went sprawling. For a second, all that I could do was lay there and *gasp*. My lungs burned, my limbs burned, and when I thought about it, I realized that my heart was beating so hard, I could feel it in my ears.

Someone shouted my name and I forced myself to my knees. I watched my breath spin the dust between my hands. It was a hurricane. I vomited.

A fist found the back of my shirt, and I was hauled bodily to my feet. I expected Firebird, but when I blinked the dirt from my eyes, I was staring into Regina's tomato-like face. She had a hand against her wounded shoulder, but the bleeding had already slowed.

"Fucking *move*," she shrieked, shaking me.

When she let me go, I staggered. Firebird was shooting at someone through the gate. The shell of Agent Rathe was already running for *Redwing*. I caught myself against the edge of the gate, still gasping, and Regina swore at me.

When she grabbed my bicep, her fingers sank deep into the muscle. I cried out as she hauled me toward the ship, half carrying, half dragging me. We passed Firebird. And when I saw *Redwing*, the engines were glowing hot.

"NO!"

The scream came from the ship. Ori had woken up, and though she leaned drunkenly against *Redwing*, her eyes were wide. She pointed at something behind Regina, her voice high with pain and despair. We turned.

Firebird was on her back, clutching her side, and the Dragon standing over her had its rifle trained on me.

22

KILL

Thirteen is the number. For BioMages, there need be no others. Their existence revolves around it, their very nature depends on it.

It is unlucky, and everyone knows it.

Thirteen BioMages changed the worlds. Despite the sheer number of them on Earth, finding thirteen with similar wills is nearly impossible. Every human is unique, and everything from their experiences to their DNA alters their power.

But when thirteen BioMages with similar wills unite, their power is amplified. One BioMage can influence up to thirteen people. Thirteen BioMages can warp the universe.

One will, one purpose: thirteen BioMages are the axis on which Unity turns.

* * *

Regina threw me onto the ship. My last glimpse of Firebird was her laying on the street, blood pumping between her fingers, eyes closed and face toward the sky. The Dragon's bullet had grazed my shoulder, and pain flashed bright when I pulled myself to my feet.

Margaret was there, standing in the hallway, hat off and under one arm. She took me by the wrist and pulled me along behind her.

"Firebird," I panted, gagging on the air. "Firebird is down."

"And down she will remain," the areologist said. "Is this the fastest you can move?"

"No," I snapped, jerking my arm free. "We need to—"

"They are going to kill you," she snarled into my face. "Move, or you're as good as dead."

When Margaret shoved me, it was with more strength than I'd given her credit for.

"We can't fucking leave her there," I argued, slapping Margaret's hand away.

"We can if we want to survive," she told me. And then, she hit me in the face with a full-armed slap. "And *do not* swear in front of me."

I blinked stars from my eyes. Margaret's hat was crumpled under her arm. She scowled at me. And then, Regina hauled Ori and Agent Rathe through the door, one under each arm. Ori was fighting her, shrieking incoherently.

Agent Rathe silently stared at nothing.

"We *can't*," Ori screamed, trying to throw herself back out the door.

Regina slammed a fist against a console.

"*Go*," she shouted.

"Firebird," static filled the hallway with Harry's voice.

"*GO!*" Regina screamed, not bothering with the console. Her voice reverberated through the ship. I stared at her, realizing that tears streamed from her eyes.

Redwing's engines roared. The ship jerked, and we all went sprawling. I could hear something outside, something like a cannon, and the ship shuddered.

I shoved myself forward, lurching down the corridor. I couldn't run, not with all the will in the worlds, but I managed an awkward, fast-footed shuffle into the cockpit. Harry sat there, a white-knuckled grip on the levers to each side of her chair, and her teeth were bared. The world turned around us, and as another cannon went off, I saw the electric flare as *Redwing*'s shields caught the hit. Radars were alive with *red*.

Ships hovered just outside of the cavern's mouth, black against the purple sky. I could hear Regina swearing somewhere behind me.

"We can't go," I shouted at Harry, catching myself against the back of her chair as the ship absorbed another hit. "Firebird is still down there!"

"Hands off," Harry snapped, eyes fixed forward.

I released her chair and fell against one of the consoles to her left. It seemed to be the controls for the ship's side cannons, and the monitors flickered black where my hands were. I twisted, staring at the growing blockade.

Regina appeared in the doorway, her eyes alive with pain, and when she saw me, her face twisted into something hideous. Harry's tendons stood out in her arms, the veins on her hands thick and purple, and when she shouted, the ship seemed to flinch:

"Get on starboard guns!"

Regina snarled, but complied. There were no more chairs, and she knelt before the consoles. When she placed her hands against the screens, they were as white as a corpse's.

"Port guns," Harry snapped, jerking her chin at me. "You know how to run Combat?"

"I might," I breathed, shaking, copying Regina as I knelt before the monitor.

It took a second. I closed my eyes, riffling through memories. It was like trying to find a book in a library that you only sometimes visited. I remembered everything. *Everything.* Every word, every color, every sensation: they were a wandering network of twisted corridors.

Redwing shook again and my eyes snapped open. My hands slapped down on the monitor and I adjusted my seat, adjusting the aim. The window in front of me shifted to the back view. Ships encroached from the sides, small guns punching uselessly against our shields. I tapped a few buttons and got a rear view. There, charging and purple, was the turret.

I took careful aim. And when I fired, it was with everything *Redwing*'s port side had. The turret took it, and I watched the purple explosion with a nasty sense of victory.

Quick as that, I knew how to operate Combat— *Martian Tech, Unity adaptations for space, patented by BioTech.* I charged the guns, fired, missed sometimes, and laid a swath of destruction from *Redwing*'s port side that had the enemy ships shying.

"Take the front," Harry said, her voice crisp and military.

I complied quickly, not even considering that she could have been talking to Regina. I switched the screen and had a full view of the frontal blockade. Harry had the engines roaring at full charge, enough to warp us out of the atmosphere, and I felt a sickly tingle of anticipation as I laid my hands on the controls.

"Ready to open all kinds of hell on them," I told her.

"Punching it," she murmured.

When she slammed the controls forward, *Redwing* screamed.

Regina and I blew apart the ships immediately in front of us. *Redwing* shot through their remains like a shark erupting from the ocean, scattering ship-bits. I immediately flipped my screen to the rear view and lit into them again.

When it was over, when we were flying over Martian prairie, I experienced something for the first time in my life. When I thought back to the people I had just killed, to the undeniable, disembodied inhabitants within the vessels I had vaporized, I couldn't remember firing at them.

I couldn't remember.

23

WILL

Most human beings are born with the inherent potential to become BioMages. Martian technology allowed us to unlock the power, whereas before it only manifested in a handful of unique cases, under extreme circumstances. Firebird's BioMage abilities were extreme because of her will.

A BioMage's will consists of two halves: determination and concentration. You have to want something, something that nothing else could possibly change. You have to believe that it is real, that it will happen, and that it would happen outside of you. That's determination.

Determination without concentration, and the BioMage would alter the world at random. Like water hurled at flat earth, it seeps and bleeds out. But if that water is forced through a narrow, rocky canyon, it becomes a river. And then...well, it's as vast and deadly as the mind will allow.

A mind without limitations, unending as the universe, is as deadly within a BioMage as nuclear weapons are without. The more powerful the mind, the more potential for the BioMage containing it. Memory, influence, and power are ideas made physical by the will of a BioMage.

I have an eidetic memory. Pain remains, vivid as the day it found me. The people who hurt me: their faces are fixed outside of my mind's eye, perfect and horrible. The way my brother's casket looked, when we lowered it into the ground. The way a blurb of static crossed the TV's screen when I watched his helicopter transport go down: I'll never forget watching it crash. I'll never forget the agony. I'll never forget that first time I saw Firebird's face, as the BioMage emerged from the wreckage.

I'll never forget the names of the people she had not killed, any more than I could forget the name of the brother she had.

This pain, it trampled my concentration as I pushed against the metal in the room. Tears found my eyes and I screamed, hands extended, body rigid. I had Regina crushed against a wall. The woman wore a lot of metal. Her bracelets, heavy and punkish, secured her hands. And her belt, with its many, many bullets, was digging into her stomach, fit to cut her in half.

Ori, I had pinned to the ceiling. She'd leapt at me, and I'd reacted. Blood pounded in my ears. I *hurt*. Everything within me was an ache of some form or another, and when I screamed, the room screamed with me.

Ships have a lot of metal in them, too, and as my concentration wandered, so did my power. It intensified on my central focus—Regina—and when I pushed against the walls, it was like they were crushing me between them. My BioMage isn't perfect. I'd been thrust into this mission before I'd had time to fully understand my own potential.

This is what I knew: every metal in the world is a magnet. Sure, that's not true. But my BioMage *made* it true. I connected metals, linking the metal in a gun belt to the metal of the floor. And I convinced them of a single thing: they *repelled* each other.

"*Jezi*," Harry shouted.

I had her pinned against her consoles, the monitors black and cool. We had landed somewhere outside of Madtown, in a canyon that she said blocked enemy sensors.

Harry had turned to me, pistol raised.

"She works with Unity," she'd told Regina.

It hadn't taken long. The big woman charged me, and I reacted. Some could argue, I *over*reacted. But, given the circumstances, I doubt that they would understand.

Now I was sweating, alone in the center of the cockpit. Regina was against the far wall, Harry to my right, and Ori dripped blood from her place on the ceiling. Tears burned within my eyes, pain writhed within my soul, and I wondered if I had ever felt so alone.

"Jezi," Harry said again, softer this time, the word less a command and more a plea.

I cried. I hadn't cried in a long, long time. Given my abilities, if I cried when I hurt, I'd never stop crying. I was tough. I'd grown up in a safe home, but within a world of vengeful competition. My mother had been the axis on which my mind turned, and when I pictured her face now, my cries turned to sobs.

"I don't know what to do," I told the worlds at large. I squeezed my eyes shut, leaned forward, and—hands still raised and power still flexing—I gasped, "I have no one to be."

And it was the truest thing I'd ever said.

My brother always believed that I knew what I was doing. Even though I was younger, I was dominant. And the thing with leaders is that if people stop believing in them, they cease to be leaders. So, I played my hand. I said I knew what I was doing, and that made it real for *me*.

BioMages do the same thing, only they make it real for everyone *else*.

"Jezi, please," Harry gasped.

She wore a single piece of metal: a gold necklace, its chain fine and strong, with a gold ring strung on it. I was pushing against it, and even though my concentration was divided in three parts, I was strong enough to cut into her throat with the fine chain.

"You'll kill me," I said, sinking slowly to my knees. My arms remained spread. My shoulder was throbbing, and I let it throb. Everything turned in sickly circles around me.

"Jezi," Harry's voice was strangled. "Jezi, we *won't*."

"Like hell."

"We won't. Please, listen to me," she was trying to work her fingers in between the chain and her throat, and I threw more will against her.

She cried out when she hit the glass of the cockpit. I could feel Regina fighting against me, but they had not been trained for this. BioMages weren't supposed to be able to influence the outside world. They had control over minds, they had control within people, but this was an adaptation like no Martian had ever seen.

And Martians, my brother used to tell me, have seen it all.

Harry was bleeding. Something in the monitors had broken when I slammed her back, and her face was turning purple. The fingers that she had managed to work under the chain were in danger of being sliced off. I heard something move behind me.

"What's going—"

I slammed my will against the voice, fear lighting a fresh surge of power. It was enough to have cut Harry's head off, and when I twisted enough to see behind me, I saw that Brute had been hurtled back down the corridor. When Jiggy hit the far wall, it was with a resounding *crack.*

Time paused for me. It's a terrible thing, when it happens. It's always important and rarely—*rarely*—good.

Jiggy shattered.

When Brute fell free of the little spherical robot, she was too small. Short and thin, her arms and legs pale, she hit the floor with a terrible *smack.* Her round, dark eyes were surprised.

Worse, the second she breathed, her lips turned a terrible shade of purple. She probably would have screamed, but her lungs didn't inflate. She rolled onto her back and began to spasm.

Whatever will was left within me shattered. I dropped Regina. I dropped Harry, and Ori fell on me. When I'd managed to untangle myself from her, I scrambled on all fours to the back wall. My hands were shaking. I pulled Brute against my chest, fear and panic tangling in a trembling ball within my soul.

"I'm so sorry," I wept, the words tumbling over and over and over. "I'm so sorry."

"Move!" Regina shouted, wrenching Brute from my arms.

And I moved. The will within me was broken. It's not a simple thing. It's the pain of loss, the anguish of waking one morning to find that a loved one has died or that a partner has left you. It *hurts*, even though no one can see the blood. Your soul is torn. And even though you pretend it's alright, even though you smile and seem like you move on, it's *anguish*. And nothing helps it to heal but time.

My time had run out. I curled in on myself and watched as Regina cradled Brute. She shouted for oxygen and from a distant room, I heard the doctor begin to clatter. I watched Harry, face flushed and neck lined in angry *red*, crawl to Regina's side.

When the doctor brought the oxygen, I thought that Brute was already dead. They worked the mechanism like they'd all been planning for this moment, and when the little mask covered her face, she drew a rattling breath.

Brute's skin began to turn an angry shade of crimson. Harry looked at Jiggy, and I saw hopelessness tremble in her eyes. I looked at the robot. It had been cracked straight through, the little cushions spilling from within.

"*No*," Regina whispered, and it was a strangled little word. "*No.*"

Her whimper caught on something within my soul. Like when you're watching a sad movie, the moment your eyes fill with tears, the moment they're about to spill and you wonder if the person next to you will notice: *that* moment, when you're too full of emotion to contain it, *that* is what pulled me from my isolated corner.

I reached Jiggy and turned it toward me. The lights around its circumference were dark, dark blue. Static ran along the line. I stared at the damage. I closed my eyes.

And I began to sift through memory.

24

JIGGY

Unity killed Mutes. People who were a threat to their empire forfeited their right to breathe. If not for my mother, I would have been executed along with the majority of my college friends. I worked the math, once.

One in ten people are Mutes.

I'd always hated math.

Unity feared us because they could not influence us as they did the rest of Earth. Empathic BioMages could not see into our minds, Inceptive BioMages could not change them. They would have had to rely on their personality alone to win us over.

Good luck with that.

When I opened my eyes, Regina had carried Brute toward the back of the ship. I followed her, Jiggy in my arms. There was a coffin-like tube there, and when Regina laid Brute in it, the little woman had turned blue. The coffin's lid snapped shut with a hiss of air. I watched Brute begin to gasp. Slowly, the horrible coloration faded.

"Firebird had been right," Harry said from behind me, her voice a painful wheeze. "We did need to keep it."

"Firebird's always fucking right," Regina growled, leaning over Brute, her hands on the glass. "Except when she brings new people to us."

The woman was too fast for her size. In the blink of an eye, she had vaulted away from the coffin, grabbed me by the throat, and heaved me against a wall. Jiggy dropped from my arms, the broken robot's innards cracking against the amplified gravitation of the steel floor.

Stars popped in front of my eyes when my head hit the wall. I grabbed Regina's wrist, but it was an instinctive gesture. My will was broken. I couldn't fix it any more than I could fix a broken heart.

"I didn't mean to hurt her," I said, tears blistering in my eyes.

"Yeah, well you fucking did," Regina snarled.

"We got her in stasis," Harry said softly. "We'll be able to fix Jiggy. We've done it before."

"You're not seriously defending this bitch?" Regina squeezed, and the edges of my vision darkened. "She brought Unity down on us. She's no different than the fucking traitor who got Maya killed. Or have you fucking forgotten about her?"

Harry went silent. It's the kind of silence that fills the whole room, the kind that chills something primal within us. It's the quiet of a hunter, ready to leap. It's the stillness of cold anger, a frosted blade.

The silence crackled as a pistol was cocked.

"Put her down," Harry said, and her voice was ice.

Regina looked at her, squeezing harder. My heels began to bump fitfully against the wall.

"You going to shoot me?" she asked, and it was an honest question.

"I don't want to, Regi. But goddamnit, I will. She's our one link to Unity. And she might be the only one who can find Firebird. So, put her the hell down."

When Regina released me, it was with reluctant slowness. I sank slowly to the floor, my eyes squeezed shut, pulling long, painful breaths through my throbbing throat. I pulled my knees against my chest. I rested my forehead on them. And I searched inside myself, wondering if there was anything left within me to feel.

"Well?" Harry's voice was soft and close. "Do you know anything?"

I looked up, and found the pilot crouching in front of me. Her eyes were quiet, her mouth thin, and I saw pain beneath the fragile surface of her flesh. I glanced at the angry red line around her throat.

"I'm sorry," I told her. "I didn't know what else to do."
She nodded.

"You still don't," she said.

"I don't think that there is anything to be done. They have her. It's over."

"They've had her before," she reminded me. "They've never kept her. But the longer we wait, the more they hurt her. If you're the key to finding Firebird, then Jezi, I'm going to get it out of you. One way," and while she didn't glance at Regina, I could sense her implication, "or the other."

"I didn't know that they were going to be there," I told her. "Rathe sent me to you, but I didn't know what his plans were—they wouldn't tell me, not when I was going to live with the most powerful BioMage in the worlds."

"He wouldn't," she agreed. "But that's not the question. I want to know if you know the location of the nearest Unity base. They haven't had her for long. They'd need to quarantine her. They know that she can penetrate their visors, and they'll want to transport her off world as soon as possible. If we let them get her to Earth, we're fucked. So, Jezi, do you know anything that can help us?"

"Just let me fucking beat it out of her," Regina offered.

Harry raised a hand at her companion, her eyes remaining on mine. I swallowed again, and it hurt. My gaze flicked to Brute, small and broken.

"Who," I started, looking to Harry's necklace, "is Maya?"

Pain flickered through Harry, a chink in her armor. I clenched my fists, eyes climbing to hers.

"She was my wife," she managed, her teeth clenched.

"She died," I said, nodding. "You were betrayed by someone."

"What the fuck does this have to do with—" Regina started.

"Your talents," Doctor Ravin said from her place beside Brute, "lie in a field more suited to hitting things, my dear." She cocked a brow at Regina. "Let her talk."

The woman looked ready to hit her, so I continued:

"It's why Firebird needed me," I said. "She knew that my contacts in Unity would get the story out. She needs support, and as an anarchist, she needs to bring down the Martian government as well as Unity. Your last…journalist. What was his name?"

"Maverick," Harry said, and it was the thinnest word.

"He tried to steal the tech from you, to sell it to Biggie," I nodded. "Somehow, Maya got in between him and what he wanted. Was she an areologist?"

The question hung in the air. I scrubbed the back of my hand across my cheek. There was blood there, and I did not know if it was mine.

"I'm not what you think I am," I told her. "I work for Unity, as I told Firebird. I did not know that Rathe would be there. If I had to guess, I'd say that he'd been tailing me from the start. Unity wanted me to infiltrate Firebird's crew. They wanted me to send Martian tech to them."

"Did you?" Harry asked.

"I did. But it was flawed." I looked at the doctor. "When they attempt to implement it, the vessel will be useless. Worse than useless—it will be combustible. If you hate Unity," my gaze returned to Harry, "you might have the beginning of an understanding of how *I* feel about them.

"They thought that they could use my brother's death as leverage. My mother did, at any rate. They were sure that I blamed Firebird for his death. It was their idea that I write about her."

"That can't be true," Regina snapped. "Firebird's notoriety grew because of what you wrote. Why would Unity want that?"

"Because they wanted to build a figure for the people. Unity breaks minds, but they are not perfect. They miss Mutes. They miss screenings. Some people slip through their BioMages' fingers, or pass inspection through flawed technology. Sometimes, they succeed in paying off the authorities.

"If Mutes are hiding from them, they will struggle to find them with BioMages alone. But if the Mutes had a figure to look toward, an idea to strive for, the prospect of freedom—and if someone who they trusted told them where to go to find Firebird...well, if that someone worked for Unity, it would be devastating.

"I won't lie to you. I've been the reason for many rebels' deaths. You cannot understand my reasons in a day, any more than I could understand your soul in a moment. When I went to Firebird that first day, it was Unity who sent me. They assumed that I would be captured or killed, depending on what she knew.

"They wanted to know where she was hiding. Her infamy had grown enough. They needed to bring her down in a spectacular way, in a way that crushed Earth's hope. They thought that they'd made me. They thought that it was time for the final move.

"But here's the thing with Unity," and I smiled. "They don't realize that the pieces they're moving have minds of their own, and that the game isn't on a board they can entirely understand. They're like BioMages. They're so used to having what they want become a reality that they forget the world never worked that way."

Harry stared at me for a long while.

"What, then," she began slowly, "is your move?"

"Firebird killed my brother," I told her. "I hate a part of her, just as Unity wants me to. I cannot change that, any more than you can stop missing Maya. But here's the truth: my brother was a fool. He believed in Unity because Unity gave him power. It was easy. I cannot forgive the person who killed him, but I *can* believe in what she stands for.

"Unity has killed every Mute they could find. They thought that there was a defect within us, because we did not react to the BioMages. Usually, that is a sign that people can *become* BioMages—it's the first step in screening. If we did not react to the serum, then we were labeled as a threat to society and put to death.

"In doing this," I smiled at Harry, and there was no humor, "in destroying what they did not understand, they destroyed themselves. There is no such thing as a Mute. There are only BioMages who cannot react to the established science. We didn't fit into their idea of the universe, and therefore we ceased to exist."

I found a tendril of will. It was deep within me, not tied to survival, but to desire. And when I pushed against the ring at Harry's neck, it was as gentle as a butterfly's wings.

"I'm a MetalMage," I told her, watching the ring move. "And since Mars never issued the same prejudice against Mutes, they have access to thousands more than Unity. They're going to come for them, now that they know. And that's why I'm here. I believe in what Firebird stands for. I hate her, but I am not ruled by emotion. It fuels my power, and I chose where that power goes.

"I do not know where they took Firebird," I tapped my temple. "But I know how to find her."

25

PLANS

There's a lot to be said for people who are united by a cause. Regina and I can work side by side for hours, so long as our wills are focused on a united purpose. It's like when thirteen BioMages connect. Their power is amplified toward a specific result.

The coordinates for Unity's Madtown base weren't hard to figure out. In fact, the second I'd found out that that was where Laurensen was taking me, I began the calculations. And while I detest mathematics, there is purpose in every evil.

Unity bases required three things. Access to moving water, an open environment, and proximity to a Martian settlement. Combined with my study of Martian terrain, there was really only one option.

"They need moving water for their power," I explained to Margaret as I used the computer lab. "It needs to be completely self-reliant, or Martian authorities would find the power drain. They prefer water over wind because turbines are bloody difficult to hide."

"I didn't ask," Margaret informed me, not looking up from Jiggy's carcass.

I glanced at her work. The little robot was coming together, thanks to the documents I'd found on Brute's computer and my memory of its design. Margaret's hands were as steady as a surgeon's, and as the leading expert in Martian technology, hers were the hands elected for the reassembly of our greatest asset.

"I'm still confused on why you needed a journalist here," I told her after a while, my eyes on the computer screen as I scrolled through the bottomless information on Unity bases. "From the way you made it sound, you wouldn't have come, otherwise."

"I am a woman of spirit," she told me. "I cannot justify murder without cause."

"And how, exactly, am I making it just?"

"Firebird's purpose is a righteous one." She sighed, setting down her tools and looking at me, her dark face lit with the ghostly glow of electronics. "But if no one knows of it, what good can come?"

"Oh, I don't know...we could overthrow the forces of evil," I said, perhaps a little too sarcastically.

"Could we?" She cocked a brow, returning to her work.

After that, I left Margaret alone.

"They need an open environment because their cloaking isn't perfect. They have a harder time with 3-dimensional projections," I told Harry, watching her as she crawled around under the monitors of the cockpit. "They prefer to burrow into the ground and create a base—kind of like Madtown. Then, they merely need to cloak the access point."

Harry didn't answer. She laid on her back under the console, carefully checking *Redwing's* controls and wiring. She said that she was concerned that one of the turret's shots had damaged the ship's integrity. But, if I were to take a guess, I'd say that she came here because being in the cockpit put her at ease.

"Why '*Redwing*'?" I asked after a while.

I was sitting in her pilot's chair, my legs crossed with a piece of Jiggy in my lap. I didn't know shit about rewiring a highly sophisticated robot, but Margaret had given the task of soldering the metal shell together. The little torch glowed in my hand as I applied it.

"Maya named her," Harry told me.

I couldn't see her face, but I heard the way she said the name and something deep twisted inside of me. I sighed. Sometimes, there is nothing to be done but to breathe out the sharpness of pain.

"But, why '*Redwing*'?"

"Because my ship has red wings."

And, after that, I left Harry alone, too.

"Unity bases need to be close to Martian settlements," I told Ori and Doctor Ravin, "because they use Martian tech to piggyback interglobal messages. They don't have the power or the technology to reach Earth with transmissions. Or, rather, they don't have the tech to push the transmissions faster than a few days. Martians perfected instantaneous transmissions after the revolution."

"I'm aware," the doctor told me.

She was carefully unwrapping the bandages around Ori's skull. She sat on the examination table, legs dangling, her hands restless on the table's edge. I realized that it was the longest stretch of time I'd seen her not actually eating something. I reached into a pocket, holding Jiggy carefully balanced on one thigh, and procured a protein bar. When I tossed it to Ori, she grinned.

"No hard feelings?" I asked, resuming my work on Jiggy.

"Baby," and she took a savage bite from the bar, "when we're done here, I'm probably going to kill you."

It seemed as good a time as any to leave Ori alone.

In the end, we took a single day to prepare. By the time Jiggy was repaired, my hands were raw from the soldering torch. Doctor Ravin procured a cooling salve and I watched them as they brought Brute out of stasis. The tiny woman went into Jiggy quickly, and when the robot whirred to life, her eyes fluttered open.

"What's going on?" she asked, blinking at us.

"We thought we'd lost you," Harry told her, smiling as she placed a hand against Jiggy's side.

Brute paused, searching around within Jiggy. Then, the little lights flared orange and she bolted toward the ceiling.

"WOAH!" She shrieked, her voice robotic and furious. "WHO THE HELL MESSED WITH MY CONTROLS?"

I'd never seen a red quite so deep as the one that whirred around Jiggy's circumference. She looked at me. And then, she shot forward and collided heavily with my chest. I went flying, my back smacking against the wall, and for a moment, I thought she intended to crush the life out of me.

"Sorry," she said, vaulting backwards. "That was supposed to be an embrace of forgiveness. But *someone*," and she scowled at Margaret, "has gone and taken liberties."

"You could increase your overall output by three-hundred percent," Margaret shrugged. "I couldn't see a reason why not."

After that, we all left Brute alone.

"If you think you're getting a weapon," Regina told me as I entered the armory, "you've got another thing coming."

"I don't need one," I reminded her, tapping my forehead.

She scowled at me. Regina didn't strike me as the tidy type, but I couldn't have laid out two suits of armor with greater care. Each had the gravity boots, a pair of pistols, holsters, and the suits that she and Ori had worn when I first met them. Along the walls, there were rifles—fire, acid, and powder—and each was locked in with its own security monitor.

"I would, however," and I gave her a smile that I'd reserved specifically for annoying my brother, "appreciate some armor."

Regina snorted.

"Why the fuck would I care?"

"Because I will prove invaluable in the base," I told her, the obviousness of the statement drawing a flare of irritation from the big woman. "It'd be a shame if someone put a hole in my priceless brain."

She paused.

"Doesn't invaluable mean not valuable?"

I stared at her. And when I started laughing, she didn't hesitate before supplying my cheek with a full-armed slap. It sent me into the table she had the armor laid out on. And, though my face was ablaze, I continued to grin.

In the end, I managed to get a set of armor from her, mostly because Ori came in and told her that if they were going to kill me afterwards, it'd be more fun if I lasted a little bit longer. I didn't know whether or not to thank her as I suited up. I settled for being content with my gains. The armor was Martian tech and bright, cherry red. When I pulled the helmet on, it surprised me by smelling—not like sweat and spit, as I'd expected—but literally like roses.

"Whose is this?" I asked, my voice too loud within the confines of the helmet.

Ori slapped the side of my head, hard enough that I tottered despite the gravity boots.

"What?"

My voice rang out of the helmet with a robotic twang. She grinned at me around a mouthful of some kind of fruit.

"Thanks," I said, tapping the side of my helmet and finding the switch with my fingers.

"Toggle it," she told me.

I complied.

"IT WAS MAYA'S!"

Ori's scream went through some kind of internal communicator within my helmet, and I wouldn't doubt if my ears had spontaneously begun spurting blood. I flipped the toggle with several panicked motions while Ori laughed, her voice booming through my skull.

Harry had us in the air by midnight. When *Redwing*'s cloaking engaged, I felt like the air around me had solidified. And after, the gravity was lessened to the point that we needed to turn our boots on. Regina—in her gargantuan, spiky, black armor—stood in the cockpit behind Harry, watching the black Martian ground beneath us.

"We look like Christmas," Ori said, throwing her dark-green armored arm around my shoulders.

"You look like idiots," Regina informed us.

"Quiet, please," Harry muttered.

"What? If you crash and kill us all, I don't want my last thought to be of being fucking silent," Ori's white grin flashed behind her helmet's dark glass.

Harry's jaw muscles bulged as she clenched her teeth.

Redwing's engines were hot enough that the air around the ship seemed to vibrate. I had a hard time determining our speed, with only the stars above us to go on, and I found myself holding my breath as we neared the coordinates I'd guessed.

If they weren't there, I was under no delusions. Regina and Ori would surely rip me apart.

Harry eased back on the controls and the ship slowed. I started to reach for the back of her chair for balance, thought better of it, and eased back on my heels instead. The coordinates ticked down on a central monitor. My eyes flicked from them as they neared zero to the windshield, where the black nothingness of the Martian prairie stared vacantly back.

"They won't be exact," I muttered to no one in particular. "It's my best guess."

We were now in the hundreds, and descending quickly. My palms were sweaty within the red gauntlets. Ori's arm around my shoulders tightened, and I could well imagine what she was about to say.

When the double digits appeared, my stomach made solid attempt to tie itself into a knot. Harry drew the controls back slowly, until we barely seemed to be moving. The numbers slowed, ticking down. And when we reached zero, I cringed, half expecting Ori to begin hitting me.

"I'll circle around," Harry said, gently.

As *Redwing* tipped, one wing dangerously close to the ground, I had to hold onto Ori for balance. She had gone still. The ship was silent. I could hear my own heart in my ears.

The air in front of us wrinkled. There was a horrible second, when it felt like someone was shoving me through a funnel two-sizes too small for me. And then, we rippled back into existence.

Beneath us, the ground vanished. In its place was a glowing, red, goddamned *spaceship*. It shuttled toward us at incredible speed, fire erupting from its tail, and I didn't even have time to scream. They were fucking launching a spaceship at the exact moment we found them.

Sometimes, my luck staggers even me.

Harry did not hesitate. She twisted her controls and *Redwing* spun. The spaceship missed us by the margin of a fucking *hair*. Harry shoved us into a dive, still twisting away from the spaceship. The afterburn from the exhaust would have ignited us, but somehow, she managed to twist around the vortex in a perfect, downward spiral.

The base's entrance was barely big enough for two ships to pass. The vertical chamber was glowing hot from the spaceship's launch, and the air around us was literally on fire. Harry put *Redwing*'s nose toward the core and bolted. I could see another ship prepping for launch, black and wreathed in fire. Harry pushed for more. Ori began to whoop some god-awful war cry. *Redwing*'s engines screamed.

At the last possible second, she twisted us to the side, whipping just in front of the second ship's nose, a heartbeat before that ship launched. We twisted into a second, wider chamber. Outside of the launching shaft, the air cooled. The lighting was soft and blue, the chamber wide and shallow, and Harry turned *Redwing* on her side, landing in a far, dark corner.

And, easy as that, we had infiltrated Unity's base.

26

INFILTRATION

My mother knew that I would die. It was the only possible result of an impossible mission, after all, and she'd always been a woman of logic. I remember the way she looked at me, when she told me that they had captured Firebird. I remember the quiet acceptance in her gaze.

Truly, knowing that your mother is willing to sacrifice you is something people just can't forget. Even without an eidetic memory. Of course, being able to pull the exact image of her expression up from the depths of my mind isn't exactly a benefit.

"That's it, then," I'd said, standing. There was an office table in between us. She wore no metal, and the desk contained none. After discovering my MetalMage ability, Unity had taken every precaution.

She looked into my eyes. Hers were unnaturally blue within her strong, black face, and her silver hair was cut short. She nodded, just once.

And that was it. I was escorted from the building, transported to where I'd parked my shitty little shuttle, and I'd driven myself to the security hold. When I arrived, I was just a journalist. And when I waited for three hours to meet the most powerful BioMage in the world, I wore my anxiety as a mask for a deep and boundless fury.

Something changes within us the day we realize that we are no longer children. It can be as subtle as losing a parent, or as depthless as discovering mortality. But, regardless, there is a shift in our souls where we thought there had already been an entire soul.

No, we are not whole. Our souls are shreds, found within the universe, torn by the souls they collide with. It's an endless cycle of love and loss and the pain of it is what makes us real. We are our experiences, built upon what we know. We are human.

And no amount of BioMages will ever change the fact that we are only as strong as we believe ourselves to be.

* * *

"The cloaking will expire when we open our doors," Harry told us, swiveling in her pilot's chair and facing Regina. "I'll get her out of here. If you can find a second exit, take it and send the coordinates to me. If not, you're going to need to get another way out of that vent, because I'm not taking her down it again."

"You did fine," Ori told her, pulling her rifle from her back.

Harry's look was murderous.

"I will *not* take her down it again, Oriana."

Ori froze.

"I've told you, *never* call me Oriana."

"And I told you, *never* ask me to put *Redwing* in danger."

"If we've adequately established that no one here listens to commands," Doctor Ravin said, ducking her head into the room, "Isn't the clock ticking?"

"Motherfucker," Ori growled, pumping the rifle like a shotgun and hoisting it over a shoulder.

She and Regina left the cockpit, arguing over which of their rifles was a better choice, and I hesitated, alone with Harry. She watched me, something unfathomable behind her eyes.

"I'm sorry," was all that I could think to say, standing there in her dead wife's armor.

"Don't be," she said, nodding once. "It fits you."

"She must have really been something," I rested my hand on my utility belt, a black band with a metal rose for a clasp. "There's a lot of personality to this."

"She was my everything," Harry said, simply. Then, shrugging, "She could afford the best."

I nodded.

"Biggie was Maya's mother, wasn't she?"

Harry's eyes widened. It was the first time I'd seen her legitimately surprised. I smiled.

"If Biggie wanted Firebird dead, she would have sent more than one ship after us in the Chryse. And there would have been scouts, when they spotted us, looking for the ship. She knew that you were piloting that shuttle. It's the only logical conclusion."

"She blames me," Harry said, gaze lowering. "And she's right to. Maya would be alive if it wasn't for me."

"You loved each other," it wasn't a question, and she didn't treat it like one. "So far as I'm concerned, that's all there fucking is to it."

"I'd rather have never loved and have her happy and alive," Harry sighed. "I'd give anything."

I hesitated. Then, I crouched in front of her, placing a hand on her knee.

"*Redwing* means too much to you for her to only be a ship. Maya gave it to you, didn't she?"

Harry smiled.

"It was her wedding gift. After marrying me, her mother cut off her funds. This was the last thing she purchased with the Overlord's bank."

I nodded, face serious.

"I'm sorry. And there isn't much I can do, but I swear to you that I'll wear this armor with pride. If there is any way to save Firebird, I will."

Harry paused. Then, she winked at me, an arrogant smile flashing across the deeper sorrow.

"If you make it through this, Lurk," and she slapped a hand against the side of my helmet, toggling the communicator so that her voice crackled through the helmet, "I might even let you back on my ship."

I found Ori and Regina waiting in the hallway before the exit.

"When we're out," I said, rolling my shoulders and activating the armor's enhanced strength, "I'm going to take point. Stay close and don't bother trying to kill people. They'll overrun us. Our only chance is if I can navigate this base."

"I wouldn't say that's our only chance," Ori brought her rifle off her shoulder and gripped it in both hands. "You've seen only the tip of the iceberg, so far as my mad skills are concerned."

"Which would be fucking great," I said, giving her a flat look, "if we were going up against the Titanic. So just do what I fucking say, okay?"

"The what?" she asked.

Regina snorted, and the sound hurt my ears within the confines of my helmet. We hesitated. Then, the big woman pulled a pistol from the back of her belt and tossed it at me. I caught it—barely—and when I gaped at her, she nudged her rifle's muzzle at my leg.

"You do anything stupid with it," she said. "And I'll kneecap you."

"Fair," I muttered, checking the magazine—*fire-based, semi-automatic, Martian Tech, hand cannon.* "Dear sweet baby Jesus," I said, giving her a disbelieving look. "You don't actually expect me to hit anything with this?"

"*If you nerds are quite finished,*" Harry's voice burst through our skulls. "*We've got a situation here.*"

"Bitch, please," Ori said, turning to the door and slapping her hand against the console. "I was born to knock heads."

She leapt through the door. The air tightened as the cloaking was disabled, and Regina snarled as she followed, gun raised. With a deep, rose-scented breath, I followed them.

27

ROSE

I was raw power.

That's what the Martian suits did; they gave you speed, strength, and accuracy. When my red gravity boots connected with the base's floor, they snapped me into motion. I charged past Regina and Ori, who were releasing all kinds of hell on the turrets closest to *Redwing*. I practically flew.

I heard Harry take the ship up. And a second later, I had Ori on one side and Regina on the other. They ran with their rifles blazing, helms flashing red from the muzzle fire. Ori used a fire-based weapon. She took out the soldiers immediately in front of us while Regina's acid-based rifle blew a hole in the door. I didn't hesitate. When I leapt through the still-melting port, I hit the ground on the other side running.

It was unfortunate, really. Because when the soldier in the hallway saw me, I didn't have time to even raise my pistol. He was already aiming toward the door, and all that was left was to pull the trigger.

Something hit me from behind and while Regina and I rolled, Ori took the soldier out with a bullet between his visor-covered eyes. No more had our momentum halted against a wall before Regina was on her feet and hauling me to mine. I blinked, disoriented, and Ori turned to start firing through the door we'd just come through.

"Keep it together!" Regina shouted, giving me a shake.

I nodded.

"Give me a second!"

My eyes snapped closed and I began sprinting through my mind, searching for the correct map. All Unity bases have a similar layout. It's a lack of creativity induced by their disdain for the arts, I like to believe.

"Right!"

I started running and they followed closely. Ori's rifle was just over my shoulder, and as she blasted away at the guards, I quit noticing them. They ceased to be obstacles in light of Ori and Regina, and they were merely distractions for me. I skidded around a corner, dropped low and let my escorts blast through another ten soldiers.

The cell block was on a lower level. I found the elevator, sprinted past it, and bolted down the stairwell.

"She'll be in the highest security," I said, taking the stairs four at a time, relying on my gravity boots. "We need to—"

I rounded the last corner too quickly, beating Regina and Ori.

The guard in front of me opened fire before I was even fully revealed. I felt three bullets hit squarely in my chest and I flew backwards, literally blown off my feet. They were powder-based rounds. My lungs spasmed, refusing to draw air. When Ori leapt over me, she riddled the guard with fire.

Regina seized me by my shoulder and hauled me up, bracing my back with an arm of steel. I coughed, hands travelling over my armored chest. The red paint hadn't even been fucking chipped.

Ori turned to us, the static prelude to a question, and I saw a second soldier round the cell block's corner. I shouted when I raised my gun, pulling the fat trigger. It *exploded*. So did the soldier's head and half of the wall behind him. The kick would have sent me flying. Instead, I bowled Regina over when the gun popped back against my face.

Ori appeared over us, her grin white. She offered us each a hand and when we were pulled to our feet, Regina had her rifle aimed just past her. She slapped my back.

"Sweet baby Jesus, indeed!" she said.

I was shaking when I began running again. We were in the cell block, and it wasn't large. All in all, it was one of the smaller Unity bases on Mars. I'd known that, and that was why I'd been so confident I'd find Firebird.

What I hadn't known, was that she wouldn't be alone.

As we slid to a stop in front of Firebird's cell, soldiers poured in through the door behind us. They didn't dare fire, not with the women in front of me. I couldn't feel my legs. I stared and, as I stared, my gun fell from numb fingers.

"Jezi," my mother said. "You're late."

28

THIRTEEN

"No," I breathed.

I don't know why I bothered denying it. My mother stood in front of me, tall and black and powerful. Her silvery hair glowed in the pale, artificial light. When she smiled, there was no love in her eyes.

Firebird was behind her, bound on her knees, a gag of metal in her mouth. She stared at me, and her dark eyes were bloodshot. Blood dribbled from her forehead. Behind her, a Dragon pointed a gun at her back.

"Is that any way to greet me?" she asked.

Her voice was as listless as I remembered. Everything about her, from her poise to her smile, was *clean*. She was as robotic as a biological creature could stand to be.

Regina and Ori had their guns trained on her. Ori's voice crackled:

"Is that who I think it is?"

"God help us," Regina swore under her breath. "That's a fucking *Yo*."

My mother, *Yo* Ruse, had taken her name from mine when Unity was born. She said it was for my own protection, but I knew better. I knew that she didn't want to be associated with me, not when she realized that I was a Mute. Very few people knew that my mother was *Yo* Ruse.

One of the Thirteen Lord Commanders of United Earth.

"I had hoped that you would bring more," my mother reprimanded, nodding to Ori and Regina. "Everyone but the pilot. That was the deal."

"Deal," Regina deadpanned.

"There was no deal," I told the room at large, forgetting that my mother couldn't hear me.

"The hell there wasn't," Ori snarled. "You fucking, lying, treacherous *bitch*."

"I didn't," I said, voice as dead as my mother's. "I didn't."

"I'd like for you all to get on your knees now," my mother said, her smile sickly.

I was the first to comply. I stared at the hidden face of the Dragon behind Firebird. There was no doubt in my mind that my mother would kill her. Doubtless, she would kill her even if we did everything she asked. I needed time. I had to think.

But I found myself drowning in memory.

"Fucking bitch," Ori breathed as she got on her knees beside me. She threw the gun down and put her hands behind her head. "Fucking, fucking bitch."

Regina was silent as she knelt beside me. She dropped her rifle without ceremony.

"Things are very simple, now," my mother said. "My dear, you know what I need."

I tapped the side of my helmet, and my visor whipped back. The air was cool against my sweaty face. I stared at her, met her gaze, and I felt the beginning of pressure against my skull.

My mother always moved slowly. She would raise the intensity of her Empathic BioMage power with the undeniable force of the moving Earth. And while it did not have the shock value of a full-on assault, the glacial pain quickly became maddening.

"Ah," she said.

Regina and Ori screamed at the same time. They fell, spasming on the floor. I did not know what people felt, when my mother began to sift through their minds, but this is what happened to all of them. Her eyes glazed with power. Her smile widened. And as the pressure against my skull increased, so did the volume of their screams.

I looked past my mother, to where Firebird was kneeling. She met my eye, reptilian eyes rimmed in red. She was burned out. Given time, my mother could fracture even the strongest of minds. And something within Firebird was broken. I could see her, she didn't have the vacant stare that Rathe had gotten when he broke, but there was pain. She was out of power.

My eyes were drawn again to the Dragon at her back. Its face was entirely obscured, body encased in the customary black armor. And yet...something tickled at the back of my mind.

"Stop," I said, looking again at my mother.

"Why?" she asked, pushing harder, her eyes darkening.

My forehead felt like it would split open. Ori and Regina began to spasm, their screams cutting off.

I moved with the quickness granted by my armor. I grabbed the gun I had dropped and pointed it under my own chin.

The pressure against my skull abated when my mother looked at me. She was one of the most powerful figures in Unity, the Lord Commander of a fucking planet, and when she looked at me, something small in my chest trembled. Still, I held the gun steady.

"What are you doing?" she asked, more curious than angry.

"You need me," I said. "More specifically, you need my *brain*. You need it intact." I gave the pistol a pointed shove, burying the muzzle in the soft tissue under my chin. "And if you don't let them go, I'm going to paint the ceiling with it."

"Jezi, my child," she wore no metal, and my eyes flickered to the gag in Firebird's mouth. "You need rest. You've been under tremendous stress, and you've done well."

"Don't," I breathed. "Just don't. You know that I'll do it."

"I know nothing of you. You won't let me in."

When she slammed her will into me, it wasn't with the gradual pace she'd lead me to expect. Instead, she shoved everything she had against me. And my mother's mind was as vast and angry as the universe itself.

I screamed. No, screamed isn't the right word. My soul *died*, and the noise that came out of my mouth was something of its anguish.

I saw Ori and Regina as I flailed on the floor. I saw them rising again to their knees, saw them watching me. I saw them look at the gun that fell from my fingers as I convulsed.

"If you would only let me in," she said, somehow both sympathetic and deadly, "your pain would be at an end."

"You know she can't," Firebird said around the gag, bloody drool dribbling to the floor.

The pressure lessened somewhat. Enough for me to have the coordination to begin vomiting, anyway. My mother half turned to Firebird.

"We are recording this," the *Yo* said. "In the next hour, your death will be spread across Earth. And Unity's power will be absolute. I want to thank you for your contribution to the cause."

The Dragon behind Firebird cocked the pistol. Ori and Regina screamed, but my mother's will spread and they were sent once more to the floor. The Dragon paused. And then, the visored helm lifted, just enough to look at me. Somewhere behind the black glass of her helm, I saw her smile. Her eyes met mine, and even through the pain, I recognized them: one green, one blue.

She fired.

My mother stared at me for a moment. And then, our gazes fell to her chest, where *red* was blossoming between her breasts. Her mouth fell open. She turned, looked at the Dragon.

When Rawn Laurensen removed the helmet, her eyes were electric.

"Did you miss me?" she asked, cocking a brow.

29

STORY

Firebird had never been successfully held by Unity, and I believe that it's because deep down, people's desire for freedom is greater than even a BioMage's will. When Laurensen shot my mother, the soldiers in the room dropped. I think that she had been holding them there, ensuring their loyalty, and when her presence disappeared, so did their resolve.

Laurensen tapped the side of her helm, and static burst through the room.

"You get the footage?" she asked.

"*You know it,*" Brute's voice filled the air. "*Now move your asses. Harry and I are coming around.*"

Regina hurried to Firebird, pulling her to her feet with the same gentleness she'd tended to Brute with. When she pulled the metal gag from Firebird's mouth, she began to cough. Ori slapped her hands down on her thighs, laughing.

"You think you could have let us in on this?" Regina asked.

Firebird gently removed herself from Regina. Her eyes were still bloodshot, but the broken will that I had seen a moment before had shifted. When she looked at me, her eyes contained the same power-imbued gaze that had first captured my soul, all those years ago.

When she offered me her hand, I was almost too surprised to take it.

"I'm sorry," she told me, helping me to my feet. "You are not a puppet to be tugged at. But when worlds hang in the balance, sacrifices must be made."

My knees were weak, my head throbbed, and exhaustion hung heavy on my bones. I looked at my mother's body, and my knees buckled.

Regina caught me before the floor did. At a gesture from Firebird, the big woman swept me into her arms. The last thing I remember of Unity's base was that the blood looked black under the artificial light.

The video of the *Yo*'s death went live later that day. Riots and chaos ensued. The Overlords, upon learning of their ultimate enemy's weakness, threw everything they had at Unity's Earth. It was war, but as short lived as a war could be. Without the central Thirteen BioMages, Unity's power crumpled. Wars broke out within Unity's own folds, and the Overlords knew exactly how to exploit it.

The power between Earth and Mars had always been a tedious balance, and the death of my mother was just enough to allow for the Overlords to free Earth.

Freed in the same way as a bullet frees the soul, I suppose. Leaderless and thinking for themselves for the first time in twenty years, the people of Earth were broken. When the Overlords seized control, it was the ruler of Olympus Mons who rose to the top. He claimed Earth, and the remaining Overlords were not in a position to argue.

All of this I found out a week later, when I at last woke up.

My mother's strength had broken something inside of me, something too unwieldy to be called entirely will. If it would have been Firebird who threw her power at me instead, I wouldn't have shattered—even though she was and remains the most powerful BioMage in the worlds. I think that it's because it *was* my mother who did it.

I know it was.

But awaken I did. And when I saw Doctor Ravin hovering over me, the first thing I said was:

"Did you have a chance to listen to the concert, yet?"

Ori threw an apple at me when I was well enough to stand, and when it bounced off my chest, she told me that we were even. Regina didn't bother looking at me. She merely moved a bit down the bench in the kitchen and gave me room to sit.

Brute collided with me in her strange, gravitational embrace, and I was pleased to see that she'd corrected the adaptations. Margaret gave me a sharp look and informed me that my article was long overdue. When I didn't bother answering, she muttered something about laziness and the devil.

Harry, I went to see. I apologized for Maya's armor, told her that I'd done my best not to get shot. She smiled that strange, sad smile at me. And then, she said:

"It's your armor, Lurk. You can get shot as often as you like."

I woke up the next morning to find Eerie's nose an inch from mine. I was surprised to find that his breath smelled much the same as a horse's.

"Of course, it does," Laurensen said when I remarked on it. "He's a fucking vegan."

She'd been sitting in the corner of my room. And when she came to stand beside Eerie, she placed a cool cloth across my forehead. I stared at her, not sure whether I should be grateful or concerned, and she merely grunted:

"Don't get used to it."

When I found Firebird, she was sitting outside of the ship. Her back was against a thick tree and there was room for me as I slid down beside her. She didn't look at me. Instead, she stared over the cliff's edge at the ocean.

"There is a ship leaving for Earth tomorrow," she said. "If you want to be on it, Harry knows the one."

I paused, pulling a strand of purplish grass and rolling it between my fingers. It stained them blue.

"I suppose security is pretty lax, now. Unrestricted travel between the worlds."

Firebird nodded.

"So," I sighed, leaning my head back against the tree. "What's next for you? I mean, now that you've brought down Unity and saved the galaxy from being bleached."

She smiled.

"Martian Overlords are no better than Unity Commanders," she told me.

"That's true. So you're going to topple the governments of the worlds and become Princess Universe?"

She cocked a brow at me.

"Excuse me?"

I smiled. We stared at each other for a minute, and she kept her will under such delicate control, I felt only the smallest breath of it.

"I plan," she said, looking again at the ocean, "on reminding humanity what freedom is. When I'm done with that," she shrugged. "I've always wanted to try ranching."

"What do cows even look like here?"

She grinned.

"You don't want to know."

I laughed, softly.

"So, overthrow Mars and Earth, destroy the governments, revitalize people's freedom, and liberate the universe. And then, start ranching demon cattle. I don't know, Firebird," and I let my hand fall on my satchel. "That sounds like one hell of a story."

ACKNOWLEDGEMENTS

———————

My undying gratitude goes out to my beta readers.
To Chris Williams, who keeps my science honest.
To Matthew Santo, who devours my books with an
enthusiasm that can't help but bolster my pride.
To Taylor Okeson, who has painstakingly edited over 750,000
of my words.
And to Don Williams, who—while not a beta reader—gave me
the wings with which I fly.

Without you, this book would not exist.
And I likely would have already descended into madness.